SILENCE. NO NOISE, NO MOVEMENT.
JUST EYES ON HER.

Samone looked away, struggling for composure. For control of the very air that clung to her with his emotions.

"Would you like to go to lunch?"

It was the last thing Samone expected. "Excuse me?"

"I said, would you like to go to lunch?"

She glared at him. *How dare he!*

He was a white man and she was a Sista from Harlem. He didn't know her life, knew nothing about her.

Lunch? He had to be joking. . . .

THE
REAL
DEAL

Margaret
Johnson-
Hodge

St. Martin's Paperbacks

THE REAL DEAL

ISBN: 0-312-96488-9

Printed in the United States of America

St. Martin's Paperbacks edition/March 1998

St. Martin's Paperbacks are published by St. Martin's Press, 175 Fifth Avenue, New York, NY 10010.

10 9 8 7 6 5 4 3 2 1

Acknowledgments

To My Dance Hall Crew: Brenda Connor-Bey Miller, my mentor, my friend; my rabbi and priestess who told me yes I could, and showed me how, when I didn't think I would. Marisa Steffers, whose kind heart, insightful thoughts and red Celica got me to where I needed to be and whose brilliant mind always had the answers. Angelos Georgios, for his insightful, pertinent, careful questions, which made me go off and find the answers, and James Miller, for all his computer help. To Bettina Bellinger Stafford, for cigarette runs and her on-call skills. The late Doris Jean Austin, who helped me focus. Shambet Israel, for pointing me in the right direction. Glenda Howard, for saying yes. Neeti Madan, for taking me under her wing. Aleta Daley, who saw something in my words, and liked it. Tara Bidwell, my number one cheerleader. J'Nea Shalom Woods, may it inspire you. And my husband, Terence Anthony Hodge, who saw the writer in me, gave me space to write, freedom to stay home, and wings to fly.

THE
REAL
DEAL

1

The morning after is a bitch. The morning after he says good-bye and means it.

You become aware that you knew he was leaving you for as long as he had. That the betrayal you sensed was real. You never finding the nerve to ask, and he the guts to say "I'm leaving you," until it's too late.

He tells you quickly, full of his concern and your hurt—nothing you can use. You realize that his heart and his dick belong to somebody else, anybody else but you. That he had been living without you for a long time. Suddenly, like magic, there stood the answer as to why he no longer held you in the midnight hour or, come morning, nothing could make him stay.

Samone had loved Max because he possessed the things she thought she needed. Max was tall, handsome, hardworking, and moneymaking. Max was single, childless and had a place of his own. Max believed in love and had shared himself with her.

It was easy loving Max. Easy for Samone to give everything she had, holding nothing back. It was one of the reasons his leaving was so painful.

Samone might have survived it better if it hadn't been a great love, if Max hadn't been an almost perfect mate. It might not have hurt so much, dragged her down so low, if he hadn't become an infinite part of her.

But he had, and now he was gone.

Their meeting hadn't been accidental. Samone's best friend, Pat, had insisted that they meet. Pat raved about Max, went on and on about his wonders . . . Max this, and Max that. ''And he's so fine, and he's so tall. And he's so intelligent and he works at a bank and he makes so much money, and girlfriend, did I tell you how fine he is? Did I tell you he's the director of mortgage down at Chase? You need to meet him. You really need to meet this man, Samone. You can meet here, at my place.''

Samone had been leery. With so much going on, why would he need a blind date? There must have been dozens of women in a five-block radius of Manhattan who were willing to get with him.

Still, the idea nagged at her. There had been no real man in her life at the time, and the fact that he was white-collar appealed to her ego. What did she really have to lose but some time? Pessimistic, Samone had gone to meet this Max.

After work on a Tuesday.

Samone had caught the uptown local, getting off at 181st Street and walking the one block to Pat's apartment on Riverside Drive. She had walked up the brownstone steps, through the foyer, and up the stairs to the second-floor apartment.

Nervous—*Could he be all that?*—Samone had rung Pat's bell, watched her best friend trip over herself letting her in, and allowed Pat to push her toward the living room.

Holding her breath—*Could he?*—smoothing things, her dress, her hair, making herself ready for the first sight of him, Samone turned the corner and saw for herself.

Her answer came as she sought words to say, as his eyes found hers, one sentence numbing her brain. *My God, yes, he is. . . .*

His presence made her own beauty seem irrelevant.

He was as smooth as a Hershey's bar without almonds, as dark as tree bark after a heavy rain. Max had Chinese eyes, a clipped mustache, and thick cinnamon-colored lips. He was tall, long limbed. And he was a Black Man.

Black men had power.

One second into their meeting Max had looked into Samone and had known all her secrets. Weeks later, after getting to know Max as Samone had known she would, she put it off as pure lust. But later she knew the real deal. Max jumped into all that she was and spun her, web tight. Samone, never stopping to consider, gave him her all.

And *zoom, zoom, zoom,* like a rocket heading for the sun, didn't they burn?

Now into week three of his absence, Samone found herself late, and still painfully in love, which was kind of silly because Max hadn't so much as picked up the phone to call.

At thirty-four Samone ought to have known better. But that didn't stop her from wondering, as she grabbed her black saddle bag and headed toward the door, Would today be the day that Max called to say he loved her still?

The train ride to work was uneventful. Samone shared a pole with six others, wedged, stuck, trying to keep her balance. Digging her heels into the floor of the subway car that challenged her steadiness with its lurching, swinging, and swaying. Subway platforms coming and going, 145th Street, 125th Street, 96th Street, Columbus Circle, disappearing like a memory.

She flipped her wrist, glanced at her watch, and saw it was ten minutes to nine. Late again. Her eyes drifted, clouded, the idea of work pressing her with bitterness.

Samone lacked the entrepreneurial skills to start her own business and didn't believe in the luck of the New York State Lottery.

No great-uncle would die to leave her an inheritance, and her parents were only middle-class. There was no land willed to her down south, and she had no major holdings in a corporation.

Samone had to work for a living and had no sights

on doing something else, so at the moment she was stuck in a job she did not like.

Seventh Avenue. Her stop.

Samone moved through the swarm, briefcases, heels, voices making erratic noises, clicking on metal-tipped cement steps, bumping against yellow-painted handrails as the office workers marched up into the brightness of morning.

Her workday had begun.

Midtown Manhattan, visceral, rushed. Crowded, unforgiving. The tide surged around her as Samone fought to keep her footing. One day they would take her, would sweep her up and carry her to the East River. Like a hurricane, the populace would take her up and drop her into the murky waters at the tip of Manhattan, because everyone had their own destination and would sooner jostle you along than step out your way.

Four minutes to nine. *Breakfast or be late?*

She allowed a two-second debate, accidentally sideswiping a couple with her bag—"Sorry"—as she made her way toward McDonald's.

She ordered an Egg McMuffin, coffee, and orange juice. Made her way down Seventh Avenue. New York City, a true concrete jungle. Rows and rows of towering buildings jammed shoulder to shoulder, jutting into the sky. Shooting straight like arrows of steel and glass, casting the netherworld below into shadow.

Samone turned left on Fifty-fourth Street. The cool air engulfed her, the deep shadows, cloistered. Not even the glass and brass of her office building managed to entice the sun. It loomed above, visible and out of reach.

She grabbed the large glass door of her office building, swinging it out on its greased bearing, not wanting to enter, not wanting to be there. Her mind jumped back in time, to those words her uncle had spoken so long ago. The words that haunted her every time she arrived for work.

You look just like a good Negro should.

You light skinned. Got that long hair. Your nose ain't too big and your lips ain't too full . . . you know how to talk that white talk, and walk that white walk. . . . Ain't no surprise they hired you, baby, no surprise at all. . . .

It wasn't her fault, and Samone realized that what prompted those words from her uncle wasn't his fault, either. It was an opinion earned, lived through. Springing from a life lived when a drink at a water fountain, a hot meal at a lunch counter, the *right* to vote, were denied him. Where half his life he was told he was less than a man. And when the sixties came, bringing changes, offering what had been denied her uncle for so long, it was all too late. The brave new world was tainted by living in the old one too long. Her uncle's past overwhelmed whatever hope there was for his better future.

His great-grandfather had been lynched, his whole family denied, scorned, and branded less than. Had been considered lacking, lazy, unworthy. Ignorant, uncouth. *Niggers.* Family history more tangible than any acts of Congress. Wasn't no laws on all of God's green earth that could make amends or reparations for the life he had been forced to live. You can change laws, but not a man's heart. *Baby, all you got to do is read the paper. Nothing changes much,* he'd told her.

Samone knew her uncle was right, no matter how many cherry black models graced the cover of *Vogue* or how many Patrick Ewings played professional ball. Samone's looks and the way she carried herself had everything to do with why she was here and not a damn thing to do with who she was.

Chalky brown, soft lipped. Bright eyes the color of cocoa. It was the dominating Chisolm genes, features passed down from mother to daughter. Samone hadn't inherited her father's dark skin, wide African-American nose, or large lips. She was a Chisolm child, as her grandmother used to say. The Lewis genes had fought the battle but lost.

Yet the idea that she looked like a good "Negro" incensed her, because it disregarded her intelligence, her wit, and her 3.7 average from New York City College.

Her current occupation wasn't the one she wanted. Ask her and she'd tell you, "Retail. I had dreams of becoming a buyer. You know. Lord and Taylor's. Macy's." She had spent her summers on the sales floor at department stores and got a BA in retail management. But neither her college degree nor her sales experience had been enough to get her foot into the buyer's world. So when the job at NBS-TV came along, Samone took it.

When she'd first started there was the thrill, the joy, the personal sense of "I am somebody." As the only black manager in personnel, Samone used to enter the hollowed halls with a sense of dignity and grace. Six months into the job she'd discovered that she had been hired as window dressing—"This equal opportunity crap. Safer to hire a black woman than a black man," she'd overheard her director saying one day.

It felt as though somebody had slapped her, hard. She'd stood there, out of sight, blinking, mouth open, bile rising. Safer? Than what? Was that how they saw her, as a lesser threat, but a threat nonetheless? Samone had stood there, six months on the job, holding her breath, a kind of fear moving through her right before the worst of it arrived.

Who she was didn't matter.

She didn't have to stay there, Samone had realized seconds after the shock let her go. In fact, she could walk right over to Harris and tell him how wrong he was. Add a "kiss my black ass" and walk away. But the consequences were too brutal. Unemployed. Her friends would call her stupid, her momma would be heartbroken.

So she'd swallowed that bitter pill. Recognized that in staying, she was giving up a large part of who she was to herself, but made the sacrifice nonetheless.

Her world shifted. Work changed forever. It didn't matter what she did or didn't. Samone stopped caring. Work became a paycheck. Nothing more. Nothing less.

Running on empty.

This was how she was feeling these days. With Max's leaving, it was all she could do to get out of bed each morning, much less be to work on time.

Like today. Samone knew she was late but didn't realize how late until she got on the empty elevator. No one was leaking coffee on the tips of her suede pumps. There were no elbows in her side, moussed hair in her face, or bad breath rushing toward her nostrils. Samone rode up quick, quiet, and alone.

With a *swoosh,* the elevator doors opened, dissuading the possibility of retreat; of calling in sick or taking a personal day.

Her high heels made no sound on the burgundy carpet as the gray wall met her view. Every single chair on the other side would be occupied.

Every day people came, résumé in hand, wanting the same thing: a chance to work in television. Whether it was to scrub a toilet or do the weekend weather, they all came to be seen by people like her.

She turned the corner, coming into view of the applicants. Found herself contemplating what life at work meant as she headed toward Merissa's desk.

Look out, baby, 'cause here I come. Yes, it's me you've come to see, late as I wanna be. . . . I am thirty plus and will probably be in this job till the day I die. But nobody gives a good goddamn about that, now do they? But here I come anyway. Moving like I mean it . . . long legs going. Hair flying in my wake.

It was all a part of the persona, her work facade. Image was everything, and Samone played the part well. Some days she didn't even know who this person she professed to be was.

To the outside world, she was flawless. Men never noticed how skinny her calves were or how big her forehead was. Not even the smallness of her breasts. What they noticed was the roundness of her behind and her hips—firm and juicy tight. It was all about sex anyway. Sex and getting some on a regular basis.

Life was about getting a man and keeping a man so you would never have to sleep alone again. From the day you played with dolls, calling yourself the mommy, making the little boy next door "Daddy," you knew what life was really about.

Yeah, Samone decided, stopping for messages at the receptionist's desk before heading to her office, I may have known what it was about then, but it don't make it any better. Especially now. Without love.

What a shitty place to spend the summer.

Samone wiped crumbs from her lips, brushed grains off her desk, and looked up as the door swung open.

She looked down at the application, checking the name, and asked, "Jonathon Everette?"

He smiled, pleasant, nervous, his whole body busy with cumbersome energy. "Yes."

She waved toward her chair. "Have a seat." Put her head down and began looking over his application for the second time. He gave a Malibu, California, address, a long way from home, Samone mused, and had owned a small production company in Los Angeles for the last seven years.

She had gotten his résumé from Jennifer over at the headhunting firm of Hunters and Associates and knew that he must have been a good candidate because they handled only good ones.

Samone took her time reviewing, feeling his stare even with her head down. She looked up, smiled tight lipped, and put her eyes back on the paper. Flipped the application, read on.

Two years at UCLA—no college degree, graduated from Moreno High in 1972, two years before she did, and received a certificate in video production in 1981; the production bug must have bit him about then.

Samone checked to see if the application was signed, noting his script was legible and that he got the date correctly. She was just about to flip the paper again when he spoke.

"Amazing."

The word arrived without provocation. The word arrived disturbing the quiet around them. Samone was not used to people talking out of turn, and it unsettled her, erasing her smile.

"Excuse me?"

He shook his head, brown bangs moving with an ease hers hardly would. Mr. Everette withdrew his eyes, studied his hands, hid a self-conscious smile behind closed lips.

"Nothing." He waved. "I'm sorry."

But Samone knew it was something. Something he'd perceived. Something personal about her. It was too early for the interview to take that turn. Too early for him to get so comfortable with her, and Samone didn't appreciate it.

She didn't have time to waste. Didn't have time for his presumptions and things assumed about her. There were six more people to see before lunch, and he was no more important, deserved no more time, than anybody else.

She looked at him, stern and unamused. Her voice arrived crisp and forthright, her tone telling him that she was about business and nothing else.

"Why do you want to work for NBS?" she asked.

Mr. Everette coughed, readying his words—rehearsed, no doubt, in front of the bathroom mirror. He sat up, shoulders forward, hands together. His eyes drifted, focused on her.

"I like the idea of a smaller network"—eyes off to the side—"I like the fact that NBS—is a relatively new company in the face of"—eyes back on hers—"the old standard networks. I feel that this newness"—eyes off her again—"will offer me a better chance to be creative"—back to her—"which is what I'm all about."

Samone sat back, one brow raised in appreciation. "One of the better ones I've heard." She gathered up his papers for the simple act of doing. Laid them aside.

"I know your qualifications, and I know why you want to work for NBS. So now I need to know a little about yourself. Tell me about what's not on the résumé."

It was her script, without much variation. Samone

had been saying those words for over eight years. She could say them backward or in her sleep, she knew them so well. The moment he began, Samone stopped listening.

Samone never listened to the tales that came hesitantly or anxiously off applicants' lips. She cared less if he had been a Boy Scout or a letterman in college. Samone didn't want to know if he was a vegetarian, a baseball fan, or a Dead head.

But a strange thing happened. His voice found the place she had gone to. Samone found herself listening, close and intently. She blinked twice, as if pinched.

"Everything all right?" he wanted to know.

"Yes, please continue." Samone switched off again but found herself right back there with Mr. Everette and what was coming out of his mouth.

Not the words, but the tone in his voice. There was a pain inside of him, something tender and still hurting. Samone found herself staring, seeking the source, a reason. Just as she thought she knew, he stopped.

Threw his hands into the air. "My life."

For the last eight years Samone had been a personnel manager. She had never been caught up like that. She didn't know herself what to say. How to set her eyes.

"Miss Lewis?"

She heard her name, but her tongue was tied. A part of her drifting, filled with empathy. Feeling warm, open. Samone wanted to pull away but could not. She locked into his eyes, captive with the golden brown irises and thick dark lashes. They reminded her of Hershey's Kisses with almond centers.

"Miss Lewis?"

Samone blinked, finding herself as she was, sitting in her office, staring at Mr. Everette. She wet her lips, disoriented. Apologized, "I'm sorry," for getting lost.

"No, don't be."

Silence. Everything coming to a halt. No noise, no movement. Just his eyes on hers, weighing and debating. Samone looked away, struggling for composure. For control of the very air that clung to her with his emotions as a smile began at the center of his eyes.

"Would you like to go to lunch?"

It was the last thing Samone expected. Surprise clouded her face, drew her cheeks down. Her eyes widened in disbelief.

"Excuse me?"

"I said, would you like to go to lunch?" There it was again. That question about lunch.

Okay, so she had slipped. This Mr. Everette had been talking about his life, and she had been drawn in. Something in his voice had pulled her. But business *was* business, and that's what the meeting was supposed to be about. Not lunch.

She glared at him. *How dare he!*

He was a white man. And she was a Sista from Harlem. He didn't know her life, knew nothing about her. How dare he ask her that?

He didn't know about her growing up singing

"Right on, Be Free"; of her wearing her red, black, and green "Black Is Beautiful" button while sporting a huge afro that needed vinegar to stay nappy.

The man before her surely didn't have a clue that she had been immersed, inspired, and baptized in blackness by the likes of Malcolm X, Huey Newton, and Nikki Giovanni; that she had been fortunate to grow up in a time when America let Black People step back and check their own selves out for all the beauty that is Black life.

Mr. Everette didn't know that as a child Samone raised a preadolescent fist high in the air at Black Power rallies and to her black-and-white TV set when the brothers at the 1968 Olympics won the gold. That to ask her that question went against every single principle she held dear.

No, he didn't know her at all.

Lunch with him? He had to be joking.

"Lunch? No, I don't think so." She reached for the phone, spoke into the receiver. Got Mr. Everette an appointment with the technical director of *New York Live* and sent him packing.

But even after he was long gone, Samone was still sitting on these thoughts, and then some.

Was still squirming (the nerve of that creep) when her phone rang.

It was Merissa, the receptionist. Was she ready for her next appointment?

"Yeah. Send them in."

*　　*　　*

Samone didn't get it. Not that it would be the first time she didn't "get" something that everybody else did. They wrote songs about the place, why? People came and laid down big bucks for small rooms and bad service. Why?

Everyone wanted to live here, why? So you could try to squeeze into a crowded subway or a packed bus?

So you could try to hold on to your bag and keep the jerk from riding your ass as the train went from Columbus Circle to 125th?

So you could subject yourself to the ever-present robber, rapist, or crack head fool out to do you harm for a buck or rage?

To see whole families of homeless people—mommies and daddies and babies—searching through the garbage for scraps to eat or soda empties to return? Is that why you come here, she thought, spying a group of tourists taking pictures of the Coliseum, speaking in a foreign tongue.

But Samone knew why, even if she didn't want to know. People came to New York City for the same reason she had gone to places like St. Thomas, Jamaica, and Mexico.

Samone had gone, blinders on, to swim in the warm blue waters and to lie on the white sandy beaches. She had gone, ignoring the tin shack dwellings and the inadequacies of wealth. She had floundered around in her vacation best, dismissing the struggling people who lived there, whose day-to-day living she *happened* on as she took island tours and explored Mayan ruins. They had come to be a tourist, and she was no different or any better.

Samone sighed; pressed on.

It was summer in the midst of the afternoon rush hour; the heat boiled the tar, and manhole covers oozed hot white steam. It was summer and it was Friday and office workers were spilling out of buildings like jelly beans from a busted bag.

Samone hated Fridays the most. They used to be fun. Fridays used to be this man, about six four, a hundred and ninety-five pounds, wearing serious New York clothes like he wore his attitude, hipside. Smelling good, flowers in one hand and her heart in the other.

Waiting there, right there by the stunted pine tree with litter in its planter.

Fridays used to be people staring at the stunning black man and woman doing their thing down Seventh Avenue.

Now Fridays was going home (a half hour commute), taking a shower, and debating whether she'd watch some porn and eat chip and dip. Fridays were her, single and alone.

There was no fine black man waiting with her heart in one hand and roses in the other. Was the reason she found herself home with only a shower to greet her as she put her key into the lock.

As her eyes lingered on the empty sofa, she knew that today would be no different from the day before. So she ditched her bag and began to take off her clothes, thinking:

Give me water. I'm gonna Baptize my Soul. . . .

2

Call Max. . . . Samone rolled over. Dared her eyes open. Looked at the clock. Still morning. Still early.

She closed her eyes, trying to find her last bit of I'm-going-back-to-sleep. But nothing in her or about her was sleepy. Her Saturday had begun whether she liked it or not. And she didn't, much.

Her best friend, Pat, was out of town. Samone had just visited her parents last weekend, and shopping was out of the question because that was all she had been doing lately.

Samone hadn't planned a weekend in years. Max did that. He'd take her for fresh seafood on City Island, book browsing at the 125th Street Marketplace, baseball games at Yankee Stadium, impromptu barbecues in his parents' Bronx backyard. "More to life than going to work and hanging out at clubs,'' he'd told her all the time.

Call him. . . .

With the sun pouring into her bedroom window and the air conditioner going full speed, Samone didn't have to go outdoors to know that it was a perfect day for the beach. That or the Circle Line.

It didn't matter, just as long as it was outdoors, in the sun, *the heat,* with Max.

She reached for the phone and tapped in three numbers before she realized, It's not like that no more.

There wasn't going to be a day at the beach and the chance to play the Beautiful Black Diva in the banana yellow bikini, Max chocolate fine gorgeous beside her. His Speedo hiding little, leaving nothing to the imagination. Slinging low below his navel to where his pubic hairs began. Those thighs, chocolate wonders, moving into developed calves and the funniest-looking feet she had ever seen. The need to have him touch her everywhere at once, riding her bones bare, under hot bright sky, the merciless sun . . .

Nope, not today, sister.

Samone put the phone back on the cradle. Considered.

But summer is our *time. How can he stay away from me in the midst of all this heat? Four weeks? He's got to be missing me. He's got to be. . . . I can call him. Call him and say dumb things like What's doing, and How about me and you get together just for today.*

I could.

Samone started dialing again. Did not stop until the last number was entered. Waited all of two rings before she heard, "Hello."

"It's me," she said as though her call were expected.

"What time is it?" It sounded as if he were still in bed. In bed and alone. Thank God. Samone knew he would not tell her no, if only for today. That he was missing her just like she missed him.

"Early," she managed.

For a second there was no sound. Then his gentle, giving laughter reached her.

"Know what you thinking."

"Oh, yeah, what am I thinking?"

He yawned, and the sound was like honey on her tongue. "Day like today, only two places you'd be interested in."

"Oh, yeah?" But Samone was only half listening. *Like you never been gone, Max. Listen to us, like you never been gone.* But he had been, for four weeks.

"Beach, preferably Jones, or the Circle Line," he went on to say.

"Maybe."

"Plans for the evening," he warned.

But Samone glided around the implications, full speed ahead with her need to see him. If nothing else, for now he was willing to spend some time with her.

"Yeah, what about now?"

"Can't do the Circle Line, and the beach's too far. Movie?"

Don't matter, Max, just as long as it's with you.
"Okay. Time?" Details were everything.

"Three. I got laundry to do."

"Eighty-sixth Street?" she asked.

"Yeah."

"Good, see you then." She hung up quickly, before he had a chance to consider that he had left her.

Four weeks ago Max had called her at work, asking her to dinner. "Rough day, I feel like a good meal," his excuse.

They'd tried a new place on Amsterdam near Ninety-seventh where everything was grilled, tossed, blackened, or sautéed. She'd had grilled vegetables (a first) and blackened chicken with pasta. One of the best meals she would ever have with him.

One of the last.

Max had swordfish and a salad. His appetite had seemed to wane as he picked over the tender white morsels and moved tomato slices around his plate.

Samone had noticed his laughter sounded loud and forced and he didn't look her in the face long. Work, she figured. Probably something about work, that place he hardly ever talked about. She had learned not to expect him to. She knew enough about the business world to know that even as a director of mortgage, there were limits and restraints put on him that no white male would ever stand for.

But Max was happy just to have the position. He had worked too hard and too long to risk it by protesting or bitching. Samone came to hate the job for him.

After dinner they'd caught a cab to her place, the ride solemn and oppressive. There in her apartment, Max had let go the words that had changed everything, forever: "I think we should separate for a while. I need space."

"Space?" Samone had repeated, confused. She hadn't understood why he would need, of all the things, of all the choices in the whole wide world, including her love, space.

She didn't have space to give. All she had was its antithesis—love. All she had was what he didn't want.

Tears had welled her eyes.

"Don't cry," he had told her, asking for the both of them. "I just need some breathing room. Four years is a long time." He had looked away from her then. "See other people. Do other things."

"What about us?" all she had cared about; all she'd wanted to know.

"We can still see each other." But he'd said it as an option, not a definite plan.

Let some other woman have what she had? It was inconceivable to her. Samone's eyes had been on fire. "I'm not going to share you, Max. I don't do that."

"Your choice, Samone." But there had been no regret in his voice. Was what he wanted, Samone had thought.

Samone had stood, folding her arms, her tears drying as her pain turned to anger. "Tell you what. When you've finished seeing other women, then you let me know, here? I'm not going that route, Max."

"Can't ask you to do what you don't want."

"Fine," had been her last word on it, even though her heart had crumpled to the bottom of her feet. Even as her mind had fumbled, imagining a future without him. Of no more fine chocolate gorgeous Max in her life, at her side. As her man.

Four years? It wasn't supposed to go that route. Four years and Max should have been down on his knees, asking her hand in marriage, not talking nonsense about needing *space*. Not running away from her love.

But Max had had his mind made up even before he spoke. He had already pondered, debated, and decided. He was already gone, his presence a formality because she deserved that much. Deserved a face-to-face where nothing she could speak would change a thing.

Samone didn't try.

She had watched Max stand, looking around him. "Can I get a bag?" he had asked. She'd known what the bag was for. Realized that he was determined to leave. That there were no ands, ifs, or buts. He was going and taking his things with him.

She had moved to the kitchen, taking out a Macy's bag from the cabinet. Had listened as he'd moved around her apartment, in her bathroom cabinet, in her dresser drawers. Listened as hangers scraped support rods, drawers opened and closed. Stayed out of Max's way as he collected his things.

Samone had stood in her living room, a cigarette to her lips, eyes clouded and unseeing as Max gathered his articles. Stunned, hurting, surprising herself that she did nothing to stop him. Determined to let him go with dignity and grace.

A part of her said it was her fault. That she had made it so by refusing to share him. But Samone knew better. It had been Max's choice and his alone.

Now four weeks almost to the day, as Samone got ready for their movie date, she wondered if he had found his space. If he had found enough of it to come back to her.

The peach lace panties seemed to burn through Samone's bag as they moved from the movie theater. She was still waiting for Max to say something about her being naked beneath her dress, but he hadn't said a thing.

Samone had come back from the bathroom and told him, her mouth wet and damp against his ear, that she had taken off her underwear and did he want to check.

He still hadn't answered, and Samone found herself waiting for his response. She nudged up against him, in love and on fire all over again, like the first time. Holding on to this time with him coming all too soon to an end.

She knew in her heart she didn't want to leave him. That she had spoken lies those weeks before; that she would see him while he saw other people.

With all the strength Samone had, she had asked Max who he was seeing these days. And with too little effort and too much ease, Max had told her. Had told her all about this woman named Zen.

Told Samone how he'd met her, at a street fair. Rambling off details like he was glad she wanted to know or that she was his good buddy and wouldn't mind hearing. Telling Samone how Zen's laughter had found him. How their eyes had met and about the gap-toothed smile this Zen had given him.

Max told Samone that he had been drawn to a woman with a face brown as nutmeg who wore seven-inch dreads. Max told Samone how he had liked this woman from the minute he saw her. That he had been seeing her since.

How could she let him go, especially now? How could she let him go off to that woman?

"Don't want to lie to you, Samone. No secrets. I don't want any secrets between us," he had confessed.

But Samone didn't want to hear the truth.

She wanted secrets. She wanted lies and myths. She wanted whoever Max was seeing to remain nameless and faceless, "out there" somewhere.

Still, this knowledge had not stopped her from going to the ladies' room and taking off her underwear. Did not stop her from trying to tempt Max back home with her or get at least another hour of his time.

With her hands wrapped around his arm, Samone rubbed against him. "Still early yet. Let's walk to Riverside."

It was all in his eyes: he didn't have the option.

"Can't, baby. Running late."

Their time together was coming to an abrupt end.

"You love her, Max?"

''No. We're just friends.''

Her throat hurt, choked on tears. ''Like me and you.''

''We're different,'' Max said, annoyed.

''Different how?'' But Max didn't answer.

We're both running scared. Me to him and him from me. Reaching the bottom of her barrel, Samone pulled out her last bit of magic.

''I still love you,'' she said, unashamed.

But her confession, this bravery of her heart, hovered and then died.

He did not want her love.

At the next bus stop, he made Samone get on the bus without him. As the light turned red and she walked on unsteady legs to her seat, Samone saw Max at the phone booth. Watched him dial a number lightning quick from memory.

And knew that another woman had stolen her smile.

3

Samone had been strong. She had battled her own demons, her feelings of self-doubt, and had lived her weekends without Max.

For the time Max had been gone, Samone had not let a second of her Saturdays or Sundays go by in despair. She had visited friends and family, gone shopping, making a gladness inside of her that Max had taken away.

Samone had been determined not to let the situation get her down. Had been determined to keep on keeping on. But when she awoke that Sunday morning after seeing Max, she had no more fight in her.

She did none of the things she normally did, get Sunday's paper, make a full breakfast. A long hot soak in the tub. Give herself a manicure.

She did manage to get into the shower, to brush

her teeth. But it was her old pajamas she slipped into and her bed where she spent the day.

Monday morning found her sleep drunk, depressed, and reaching for the phone to call in sick the whole time she was getting dressed. Even as she rode the elevator up to her office, she considered turning back around, walking out the lobby, and finding a pay phone, calling to say she wasn't coming in.

But she got off on the fifth floor as she did every morning and went into her office. Sat herself down— *I'm here now, aren't I?*—and saw four applicants.

At lunchtime, instead of ordering in, Samone ventured out into the day. She headed toward Broadway. Stopped at the deli. Bought sesame noodles, chicken fingers, and broccoli with garlic sauce. Decided on an Arizona iced tea to wash it down.

Back at the office Samone stopped by Merissa's desk to retrieve her messages and looked them over quickly. Three previous applicants, her girlfriend Pat, and a Mr. Everette, with an in-house extension. *Who the hell is that?* She glanced at Merissa and knew that this was going to be a "Merissa moment."

"Merissa moments" were those times when a simple question was taken like a slap in her face, and Merissa stared at you, hating you with every breath she took.

"Merissa moments" were common with all the personnel managers, so Samone didn't feel singled out. Still, she tried to avoid them.

Two years ago, when Merissa was hired as the receptionist, Samone had thought, Finally, somebody I can relate to. Merissa was Hispanic, but her skin was dark and her hair a smidgen above kinky. It was enough for Samone to consider her a comrade. She realized that Merissa was a sister trying to make it just like she was and had welcomed her with open arms. She'd even taken Merissa to lunch the first week. For a whole year they'd laughed and joked and talked shop in the ladies' room when no one else was around.

But all that changed.

Merissa started treating Samone the way she did everybody else—with borderline hostility. Never enough to be written up, but enough to know that Merissa wouldn't throw her a life preserver if she was standing on the deck and Samone was drowning.

Samone had tried to get Merissa to talk about it, but Merissa's response was so hostile that Samone gave up. Decided that if that was the way Merissa wanted to play it, so be it.

The air crackled every time they shared the same space. Like now, with Samone looking at the message and Merissa alternately.

The last thing Samone wanted was to ask Merissa anything. Things had become so funky between them that just the sight of her made Samone's adrenaline race. Merissa was a receptionist. Now how hard could that be? What was so hard about taking a name, a number, and a brief message?

Samone flipped the message in Merissa's direction. She saw Merissa flinch, but that was all. Merissa kept on typing.

"He didn't leave a first name?" Samone asked indignantly. The unspoken question being "How come you didn't write one down?"

Merissa kept on typing. "No."

"Well, what did he sound like?"

"White," Merissa answered, matter-of-fact.

Oh, is that supposed to be funny? You silly ass. Don't you know you're just adding fuel to the let's-get-rid-of-Merissa fire? Don't you know nobody around here wants you? And you're gonna play that with me? You ignorant ass. . . . Well, you keep going the way you're going and soon you'll be gone. You want to play this game, you go right ahead. Ain't no skin off my back.

But in many ways, it was.

Negative energy would always be negative energy, and it took energy to be standoffish and bitchy, and Samone was getting tired of the game. Had considered taking Merissa to the side and calling a truce. Considered saying, "Look, we're supposed to be on the same side. Let's be friends." But Merissa's fingers were flying fast on the keyboard, and it was obvious she didn't care about Mr. Everette, Samone, or anything else that had to do with the office. So Samone went to her office, checked the extension in the company directory, and saw a Jonathon Everette on the *New York Live* show.

It came back to her in a flash. That white guy she'd interviewed. The "let's do lunch" guy. Samone crumpled up the paper into a tight ball and scored two points as it fell in the wastepaper basket.

She had had enough of men, regardless of what color they were.

Sleepy.

Samone looked around her, the clear empty plastic container turning her full stomach. *Ate too much.* She glanced at her wall clock, one o'clock, and longed to be in kindergarten. She was full as a tick and wanted only to lay her head. To doze, give in to the sleepiness that settled along her spine, that drooped her eyelids.

Samone yawned. Looked at her desk. Looked at her closed door. She had half an hour before her next applicant. Twenty minutes would do it.

Samone pushed aside the pile of papers.

It would not be the first time she'd napped after lunch. She picked up two paper clips and tossed them in her drawer. Moved her stapler and tape dispenser to give her more room. Was about to lay her elbows—a pillow for her head—when there was a knock on the door. Before Samone could even ask, "Who?" he stepped into her office.

She looked at him expectantly, but when he made no move to speak, it clicked.

This was Mr. Everette. This was the new ofay from upstairs who had left a last name but no message. Samone knew one thing: This had better be about business.

"Busy?" he asked.

"Mr. Everette," Samone stated.

"Yeah. You probably don't even remember me." Her blank stare told him that, in fact, she did. But she wasn't the least bit impressed, and he could have stayed his butt right where he came from.

"Vaguely," Samone answered matter-of-factly.

She began putting her desk back in order, no longer sleepy. Awake, wired. Mistrustful of Mr. Everette, who took a seat, unoffered.

Samone felt like telling him to get the hell out. That she had work to do and he was just wasting time. That he was a white mutherfuck with no business with her, and he had a hell of a nerve coming uninvited to her office.

"Something I can help you with?" Samone finally asked, his silence prodding her.

"I had called you earlier, to see if you wanted to do lunch."

Hadn't she told him no the first time? Her eyebrow raised. "*Do* lunch?"

"Yeah. You know. Me, you, eating something together."

Words jumped her tongue, all of which she bit. After all, she was at work, and he wasn't that damn important.

"No. I don't think so. . . . I have someone waiting. Anything else?"

He watched her. His eyes were different today; hints of green speckled the gold and brown, tiny explosions of color that seemed determined to seek her soul.

Mr. Everette stared, giving her the willies. Hiding nothing, not his designs, not his purpose, not anything. If Samone had any doubt about his intentions, she didn't now. This was not about business, this was about her.

He continued to look, and Samone found herself looking back. That part of her that was curious, that responded to a man's attraction of her, taking a closer look.

He *was* handsome, in a different *white* sort of way. (*A white boy? . . . Could I?*) Tight jawed and sparkling eyes, summer or heredity giving his skin an olive tinge. His nose was a bit too crooked, but that didn't matter.

Against her will and on their own accord, her eyes drifted to his arms and saw how his biceps strained the material of his shirt. Noticed how full his thighs fitted into his Dockers and that his loafers were shiny, oxblood red with leather tassels.

There was little hair around his wrists, and Samone knew his chest was smooth. Wondered if his nipples were small and the color of mango.

"You look so much like her."

Her? That flipped Samone's switch. Threw her out of her moment of scrutiny and the thin line of possibility.

"Who?" she challenged, because there was no acceptable answer. Samone was an individual. She was "like" nobody else.

"Yvonne. My lover."

Samone blinked, tripped up by his response. Gave it all of two seconds of thought: *He didn't really say that, did he?* And when she realized that was exactly what he'd said, she laughed.

"Oh, and next you're gonna tell me that she's black, too."

"She is."

Her laughter was cut short. In all the thirty-something years of living and seventeen years of meeting men, Samone had heard a lot of things. Men told all sorts of lies to get into your panties. But this was the granddaddy of them all.

Her funny bone was tickled as it hadn't been tickled in a while. *Him and a black chick? Get the fuck outta here!*

"You have to be lying," she managed, wiping her eyes, not considering her eyeliner.

"Remember the interview? I was sitting right here and you were reading something on your desk. I said, 'Amazing,' and you looked up like you wanted to have my head. Remember? . . . It's because you looked so much like her."

Samone remembered. Remembered how it annoyed her, his speaking out of turn like that. That one word coming out of nowhere. Still, she found it hard to believe.

She looked at him sideways, calling his bluff. "Do you have a picture? I would like to see this person who looks like me."

Mr. Everette got his wallet and gave her a snapshot.

Samone looked at it closely. Drew her own conclusions.

Well, we're both black and female. So I guess that's why he got confused. I don't look nothing like this woman. She's two shades darker and about two inches shorter. She's got me by about ten pounds, and, well . . . my hair's real.

Samone handed the picture back. "Well, we're both black and female."

"You don't see any other resemblance?"

"Nope. None."

Mr. Everette studied the photo. Looked back at her. "The eyes, around the nose?" he offered, fingers busy over the glossy picture.

Samone shook her head, watched as he tried to hide his disappointment, handling his defeat well. Samone liked that. She paused, curious.

"What's she like?"

And Mr. Everette told her.

He loves her. I can hear it. I can see it. He misses her. That touched Samone in places she had no intention of getting touched. It dissolved her anger and made Mr. Everette, *Jon*, human. Most men wouldn't show their vulnerability. Samone forgave his conceitedness. Became curious about a man leaving behind a woman he loved so much, even if she knew why. *Men are fickle asses. They hardly got anything right.*

"So why did you come to New York without her?"

"I've asked myself that question. . . . You know when you were little and the teacher asked what you wanted to be when you grew up? Well, this is who I wanted to be. Since my first trip to New York, when I was eight, I knew I wanted to live and work here."

"And I guess she didn't."

Jon shook his head, the corner of his mouth turned

down. "Won't even consider it . . . Malibu's her life."

"So, how was it?"

He gave her a puzzled look. "What?"

Samone shrugged. "You know. You and a black woman."

He looked confused, then insulted. There was a sting in his response. "What color is love, Samone?"

It caught her off guard. She felt as if Jon had peeped at her card or had known her past. It was time to cut the topic to the quick.

She looked away. "You're asking the wrong person."

But Jon refused to let it go. "No, I'm asking you."

Wait a minute. Hold up. How in the hell did we get to this? Asking me questions like he knows me and has the right to. Her confusion gave way to hostility. Samone gave him the once-over and decided he was just a white boy taking up her time and getting into her business. *I don't know this man from Adam. . . .*

It was her office, and she was about to throw him out.

"You on lunch?" Samone asked, her voice cool as a Popsicle.

"No. You know I'm not."

The air sizzled. "Then I suggest you get back to work, Mr. Everette."

Jon waited for her to crack a joke or give a smile, but Samone did neither.

"Just like that, Samone?"

Samone felt the slight but didn't flinch. Her gaze

was steady. "Just like that." She looked away. Picked up her phone. Punched four numbers.

"Merissa, send in the next applicant."

Samone never looked up, even as he lingered at the door.

And when the door closed, Samone was glad. Glad that he was gone. Because Jon, *Mr. Everette,* the white boy from Malibu with the superserious find-your-soul-if-you're-not-careful eyes, scared her.

Scared her silly.

4

Samone moaned once. Moaned twice. Touched the wetness between her legs. All day she had waited for this moment. Since lunch, the need to come—hard, fast, and alone—had been with her; in the mild throb in her belly and the hardening of her nipples.

Waiting. To touch herself for the pleasure, for the moment when her orgasm was fierce and upon her.

Bare breasted and legs parted, blue lace panties clinging to the wetness of her crotch . . . *yes* . . . *oh, yes* . . . soft brown flesh quivering, her fingers urgent between her thighs.

The phone began to ring. Samone couldn't move to answer, could not stop the sweet promise that was swelling within her. She arched against her own fingers, the ringing phone shrilling for the second time.

"Unnnh . . ." Her body strained taut, held rigid as

the fire swept up through her, taking her up in sweet surrender. Her orgasm arrived as the phone rang a third time.

Samone sought air, the smell of her sex heavy and potent.

One more breath, then I can answer.... She opened her eyes, her hand riding the gentle rise and fall of her belly.

Just one...more...breath. She rolled onto her stomach, her uterus contracting in the aftermath.

One more.... She reached for the phone, *okay...* picked up.

"Hello," she managed, her voice husky.

"Samone?"

Who is this?...

Samone got up. Shivered. Realized she was half-naked. "Who is this?"

"It's Jonathon...Jon."

But the name meant nothing to her. Who was this white man saying her name as though he'd known her all her life?

"Who?" Samone demanded, hearing street noises in the background.

"Jonathon Everette. The guy with the girl who looks like you."

"How did you get my number?" Because it was certainly unlisted.

"A reliable source," was all he said, his voice amused.

"Don't call me anymore."

She hung up and rolled onto her back. Didn't realize how hard she was breathing until she became aware of her diaphragm going up and down.

She wrapped the comforter around her quickly, with a fear that went beyond a stranger calling.

Ring . . .

"Hello." Her voice was exasperated now. Samone knew he'd be calling back, and from the onset she wanted him to know she did not appreciate it or him.

"I know you told me not to call anymore, but I have a damn hard head."

"What do you want?" He had a lot of nerve, was all she knew.

"Just to say hi."

"Well, you've done that. Anything else?"

"The truth?"

What a silly ass-fucking white boy. Shit . . .

"Yeah, tell me the truth," like he really had some great message that she could use.

"Well, I'm new in New York and don't have many friends. And you seem like a nice person. Thought you might like the job."

"Sorry, but I already got a gig."

"The pay is good."

"I'm sure."

"Listen," Jon began. And for all the tea in China Samone knew she should just hang up, but a part of her was fascinated with his nerve and wondered what he was going to say next.

She dared him to come out with something she could use. "Yeah?"

"On the serious side, I came by your office a hundred years ago, and for a while, it was very nice. I told you all about myself, and then wham! You just cut it off. Why did you do that?''

It wasn't what she'd expected. She had not expected him to play so dirty; to use the truth against her so effectively. But Samone got down to her own twist of the facts.

''First off, I didn't cut you off. You were sitting around my office, bullshitting on company time. All I needed was for my director to come in and see us running our lips. That's why I did it.'' It sounded good to her.

''Were you worried about your director or maybe something I'd say?''

''I don't know what you're talking about.''

''Of course you do, Samone.''

He was challenging her. And that was one thing Samone could never let slide. Not only was he calling her a liar, he was trying to insinuate that she was afraid of him, which she was.

''Look, I don't know who you think you're talking to, but let me tell you some—''

''Five cents, please. Please deposit five cents for the next five minutes, or your call will be interrupted. Thank you.''

He's so much as called me a liar. He ain't getting away that easy. Before she could consider it, she was asking about change.

''You got any change?''

''No . . . only had two quarters.''

''Five cents or your call will be interrupted.'' The

electronic voice wasn't even saying "please" now. They'd be disconnected for sure.

"Well, give me your—"

"Huh?" Click. Dial tone, and Jon was gone.

Samone sat up and looked around. Tried to remember where she had been; where Jon had taken her in those brief minutes.

She didn't know. All she knew was she was pissed.

Who did he think he was, calling her at home, saying she was afraid of him? And how in the hell did he get her number?

Samone was incensed, outraged. Livid.

It was a while before she remembered she was half-naked.

They had been best friends since high school. But it hadn't started out that way. Back in the ninth grade, Patricia Robinson considered Samone Lewis a long-haired high-yella stuck-up snobby bitch from Sugar Hill.

Pat had it in for Samone back then. Samone would be walking down the hall and Pat would say something smart. Would purposely get in Samone's way and dare her to move around her, Samone going the other direction, even if it meant being late for class.

Silver bangle bracelets had brought an end to the hostility.

Samone, tired of running from the slim, dark-skinned sprite name Patricia Robinson, who had her cornered in the locker room one day in gym, decided she would stand up to Pat.

Samone had realized that she was at least three inches taller and maybe ten pounds heavier. Samone, known for her stubbornness and her inability to compromise, decided that she would do as much harm to Pat as Pat was planning to do to her.

"What do you want from me?" Samone had asked that day.

Pat had looked at the eight or so silver bangle bracelets lying quietly on Samone's tan arm and decided they would do for the time being. She could always kick Samone's ass later.

"Your bracelets."

Pat had been ugly then, ugly and mean. She wore her hair short and slicked back and had a slew of acne all over her face. Pat never smiled, but she laughed wickedly all the time.

Samone hated her. Hated her for her ugliness, her bullying, and for hating so much. She just knew Pat was a stone cold projects girl who'd have a baby by her junior year and be on welfare by her senior.

Samone just knew that Pat was the type of girl her mother warned her to stay away from, and now she wanted Samone's bracelets? Samone opened her mouth, ignoring the trembling of her legs.

"No. You can't have them. My father gave them to me . . . they belonged to my grandmother."

"Then I guess I'm gonna have to whup your ass," Pat concluded.

And Samone, still scared, said, "I guess so. Come on."

She hadn't fought since sixth grade, but she threw up her hands anyway.

Surprised Pat hesitated, not believing this prissy-ass bitch was really going to go to blows with her.

''What?'' she asked, feeling the crowd of spectators pressing up against them.

''I said, come on. You so bad. Come and kick my ass.''

Samone was tired of being afraid. She had been dodging Pat since the beginning of the school year. She might die trying, but she was going to try her best to fuck Pat up in the process.

Samone swung, refusing to let Pat swing first. But the gym teacher came by and grabbed Samone just as her fingernails were about to make contact with Pat's ungreased face.

Later, as they sat in detention after school, with Pat giving bad-ass looks but nothing else, and Samone fearful for the real ass whipping she was going to get as soon as they were let out, they had a chance to think; to settle their rage.

Pat, never thinking Samone would take her on, found a new respect for the stuck-up light-skinned bitch from Sugar Hill. Samone realized something was going on when the school door closed shut behind them and Pat didn't jump her.

For the first block they walked in silence: Samone scared and breathing hard; Pat checking out this chick who had challenged her.

At 103rd Street Samone had to catch a bus and Pat a train. They stood at the red light, waiting, each eager to get away from the other. When the light changed and Samone went to step off the curb, she heard Pat say:

"That's really cool. Those bracelets being your grandmother's."

Samone, still scared, did not respond. She was just glad she was still intact.

The next day at school, Pat smiled at her. Samone ignored it. But then the next time Pat smiled, Samone smiled back. Eventually they started saying hi, and the rest was history. By Christmas Pat was sleeping over, and the Robinson apartment on Riverside Drive ("No, Pat isn't a projects girl," she explained to her mother, "I just thought she was") became Samone's second home.

Years later they were still the best of friends.

"Patricia Chadaway, you'se a bigot."

"Bigot hell, Samone. A white dude? And you know what he's after." Which was a typical remark for her best friend.

"All we did was *talk,* for God's sake."

"Yeah, for now. But what about later?"

"Oh, please, he's got somebody in L.A."

"So why do you sound so smitten?"

" 'Cause I'm still trying to figure how he got me talking, and why I got so pissed when we got disconnected."

"He got your goat, huh?"

Samone smiled. "He certainly did. Just wait till I see him again."

"He asked you out?"

"No."

"So how you gonna see him again?"

"He works upstairs from me. I'll run into him one day."

"And if you don't?"

"I know I will. Then I'll tell him about himself."

"Samone done jumped the fence."

"I told you, it's not like that. He's got somebody. And she's black, too."

"But how do you know she's really black? Nigga could be lying."

" 'Cause I saw a picture."

"He could have swiped it out of a magazine."

"Now why would he do that?"

"For the same reason he calls from a pay phone with no spare change. To get into your drawers."

"Oh, shit, get the fuck out of here."

"I'm telling you, Samone. When a man is interested, it ain't 'cause he digs your intellect, or is attracted to your mind. It's 'cause he likes them boobs and your ass. It's a visual thing."

"Oh, and you're the expert."

"No, but I know that a line of a man's thigh was enough to make me want to speak up."

"Can we talk about something else?" Samone asked, waiting for the light to change.

Dusk had come. Life oozed around them in the flicker of the sulfur street lamps and the music that crept from open windows lining the avenue. Teenagers nodded their heads to the latest jams of Dr. Dre and Snoop Doggy Dogg. Samone, hearing the music, wondered what ever happened to the good groups from her youth, like BT Express and the Delfonics.

They took a moment to look around them and saw the changes that had come to Harlem. Renovated brownstones gone co-op, offering eat-in kitchens and twenty-four-hour security, for a price. Working fireplaces and parquet floors, for a price. A price that left out a lot of folks that had lived in Harlem before anyone downtown even cared about what was happening uptown.

Harlem used to begin around 99th Street. But with the onslaught of the yuppie dollar, Harlem began to look better and better, and the boundaries became very vague. There used to be a cultural bookstore on 125th Street called the Tree of Life, but that was before someone decided what Harlem needed was a luxury hotel.

They revitalized Amateur Night at the Apollo, and the price of rent went up for stores on 125th Street. Korean grocers took up shop where the number spots and after-hour joints used to be. Lifetime residents faced eviction.

Pat's eyes studied the huge blue-and-white sign that was advertising co-ops for sale. She sucked her teeth, disgusted.

"Just what we don't need."

"What's that, Pat?"

"Another damn building going co-op."

"Yeah. They're trying to convert my building."

"Oh, honey. You know they been after mine for the longest. Riverside Drive? Are you serious? I just hope Mr. Jenna holds on for a little while longer. At least till Shamika gets into high school.''

"Pat. We're talking a while from now.''

"Well, Mr. Jenna is only seventy. So if God willing, he'll make it till then. His sons don't want it. They'd rather sell. Don't know what I'd do if I had to give up my apartment.''

"They'd definitely up that rent. What with a view of the Hudson and two bedrooms, plus a dining room? Honey, you'd be paying outcha ass.''

"Tell me about it.''

Without notice or effort, their sneakers fell into an unhurried rhythm, rubber soles meeting the pavement with a gentle ease. Shoulders so close they touched; eyes straight ahead. The moment shared, complete.

"Thanks for taking me to the movies,'' Samone began.

"Hey, what are best friends for? No sense in you moping around waiting for Mr. Scutter.''

Samone's head snapped in Pat's direction. How dare she even speak the name in her presence?

"Who?''

"You know. That man you loved so much. Max.''

"Don't even mention him.''

Pat snorted. "Well, that's what you get for taking off your panties in a public place. Hell, I would have run, too.''

Samone laughed, tickled, embarrassed, annoyed.

"I swear, Pat. Can't tell you shit.''

"You call him?''

"No, why should I?''

" 'Cause you love him. And he sure as hell still loves you. Though he can hardly tell it from hanging around that nappy-headed thing."

"Who, Zen?"

Samone had waited for this for a long time. She wanted to, needed to, talk about the woman who had taken her place. To talk her down, tear her up with words and gestures.

But Pat was Max's friend, too, so Samone didn't feel right bringing it up until Pat had.

"Ain't that some mess? *Zen.* What kinda name is that?"

"Have you seen her?" Samone asked, unable to hide her curiosity. Wanting to know more about Zen than the dreads, the gap, and the laughter that had snared Max all too quickly.

"He was my friend first, remember? And yeah, I caught a good enough look."

"Well, what's she look like?"

"Big, brown, and round. Got these dreads and a gap. A good size eighteen, if you ask me." There was disgust on Pat's tongue, and it made Samone feel good.

"Size eighteen?" He never mentioned her size. "Max?"

Pat nodded, relieved to tell Samone.

"Guess he wanted something different?" Samone asked, not expecting an answer.

And Pat, being the good friend that she was, didn't give one.

*   *   *

Apartments were like people. They had mood swings, too. They told you how they were feeling in the way a magazine was left on a table or the angle of a chair. Samone felt as if her apartment had been holding its breath, awaiting her return.

I got the willies, she thought, turning on lights as she made her way down the short hall, past the kitchen and the living room. Her sofa, forest green chintz, shone beneath the overhead light. Her pale wood bookshelves, full of hardcover books, paperbacks, brass objects, and photographs, cast a long shadow across the floor.

Most of the photos were of Max. Samone had yet to remove them, because once she did, she'd have to face the fact that he was really gone.

With the air conditioner off, the whole apartment was hot and stuffy, as though nothing had moved around inside for a long time.

With her heart beating double time, Samone dialed the number, letting her worst fears run wild.

"Hello?"

It was what she wanted, wasn't it?

"Hi," she began, her own voice tiny and surreal in the cloistered silence.

"Samone?"

Was he surprised? Had she really caught him off guard? Hadn't he felt her thoughts since forever; since the last time they had spoken—the movie date with no panties?

"Yeah. I just left Pat. We went to the movies."

"Was it good?"

"Pretty good."

"So how have you been?" he asked.

"I could be better," she offered matter-of-factly.

"Sorry to hear that."

"Yeah, Max. I bet you are."

"You called me, remember?"

So she had. Samone let go of her anger. Sighed. "You're right."

"Glad you did." Hesitation. "Been thinking about you."

"Really? Ain't Zen keeping you busy?"

His words were measured. "Like I said, Zen is just a friend."

"Oh, yeah, like me and you, except you see her a whole lot more than you do me, right?"

Max chuckled, a tiny sound not meant to be shared. "Samone, Samone. Still the same."

"Who else am I supposed to be?"

A pause, and she knew something was coming. Something she wanted. Was not disappointed. He could still push her buttons.

"You busy for the rest of the night?"

There was thunder in her ears. "Nothing beyond doing my hair."

"Can I come over?"

Asking? This was a new Max, and it gave her an unexpected advantage. Gave her room to flex her muscle. "I don't know, can you?"

"Look, I miss you and want to see you. Now if you don't want me to come over, let me know."

And men really needed to change their lines. They

really needed to learn how to ask without trying to come off like they were doing you a favor by sleeping in your bed for one night.

Samone never answered him. 'Cause Max knew her, from A to Z.

Later . . .

Samone lay in the dark, sweat making tiny rivers over her belly. Max, stomach down, nudged his nose against her pillowcase, indulging in the smell of her.

His voice, deep, disturbed her quiet. "What are you thinking about?"

"About us."

"And?"

"Nothing, Max."

Samone rolled away onto her side. The sheet, half-draped, bared her back and shoulders. Max studied her in the darkness. Knew she was waiting for all sorts of things now: his touch, his hand to pull her to him. His mouth to nuzzle her or speak promises.

He reached for her. "Samone."

"Yes."

"It's not how I want it. Me running in and out of here like this. You know that."

Samone turned and looked at him, her eyes soft with hurt.

"Max, I don't know nothing. All I know is you're here now. But what's gonna be the story tomorrow? In the midst of so much sex, we never got the chance to discuss that part."

"Would you have preferred that I not come?"

"Would it have made a difference what I 'preferred'?"

"Yes, Samone. It would."

"Well, I would have preferred we never broke up in the first place. But it's too late for that, isn't it?"

"Samone, I—"

"Drop it, Max. Just drop it. . . . Look, you spending the night? I got work tomorrow."

Max could have left then, but love was never that simple.

Summer moved on, bringing with it the kind of heat that everyone bitched about but longed for when winter came on too strong.

Good moods had gone the way of jackets and long-sleeved shirts; they were packed away until after Labor Day. Summer, mean spirited and relentless, had no intention of moving along any time soon.

Any place that didn't have air-conditioning was a no go, and the electric company made a lot of money that season.

Max didn't call, and Samone, not up to any more one-night stands, didn't try to reach him, either.

Then one day her office phone rang.

"I can't believe you let me get away with that," he began.

"Jonathon?" Till that moment her showdown with Jonathon Everette had been forgotten.

"I really thought you'd call me back by now. Guess it just proves my point."

"What point is that?"

''You're afraid of me.''

Samone put force behind her words. ''Of you? You can't be serious.''

''Then why didn't you call me back?''

''I don't have your number.''

''You know where I work.''

Samone laughed, a free thing that escaped her lips before she could think about it. *He really is a silly-ass white boy.*

''Okay, you win.''

''Admitting defeat? *Not* Samone Lewis.''

She smiled, her face muscles moving in a way she hadn't felt in a long time. Smiling. Feeling good. When was the last time she had?

She shook her head in surrender, surprised and flattered. ''Listen, I really have to get back to work. Is there anything else?''

''Lunch?''

That word again. But the very idea tickled her. ''Didn't you ask me that twice already and I told you no?''

''That was then. This is now. We can walk to Central Park.''

''Walk? Are you crazy? It's five blocks, and it's like a hundred degrees outside.''

''Fine, we'll take a cab.''

''A cab? I can tell you ain't from New York.''

''So, is that a yes?''

''I don't even know you. Why would I want to go to lunch with you?'' Which was a half-truth she didn't have to confess to.

"Look. We take a cab to the park. Get some hot dogs and a park bench. Rap for a while. After that, it's your call."

"But why would I even want to go to lunch with you?"

"Because I'm intriguing as hell."

That he was. "Try again."

"Because somewhere deep inside, you want to."

Peeping at her card. Samone found herself fascinated, a secret she would surely keep. "I don't know about all that."

"Yes or no, Samone."

"No."

"Chicken."

"I'm not afraid of you." But she was.

"Prove it. Go to lunch with me."

And there it was again. The challenge. The need to meet it sprang up in her like wildfire. What was the harm? Lunch with another human being. When was the last time she'd done that?

"Fine. Meet me in the lobby at exactly twelve-thirty. You're one minute late, and the bet is off."

"I'll be there. I'll be the white guy."

"Oh, yeah, like that's not all we have in this place."

"Are you complaining about the hiring practices? You know, there's a Ms. Lewis in Personnel who's very black oriented. You should give her a call."

"Jonathon. Get off the phone."

"Call me Jon. . . . Twelve-thirty. Don't be late."

"Oh, I won't."

A part of her said, *Watch him.* That he had a whole bag of tricks up his white sleeve. But she fluffed away the warning with a suck of her teeth. Wasn't nothing he could do to her. She was a Sista from Harlem and he was just a silly-ass white boy on her trail because he had nothing else to do. But he was funny as hell, and Samone knew she was definitely in need of laughter these days.

So lunch became an almost daily thing. And it was cool and sort of hip. He was something to look at, and they got looked at often. But Samone really didn't care, because there wasn't anything to it but lunch and laughter.

Yeah, she thought, I can hang with this for a while.

And then it was fall, Samone's real season, where even fast-paced New York mellowed. Jazz clubs did record business, and city dwellers began taking trips to Central Park and upstate New York to witness the turning of the leaves.

Fall, where the days were hot and sunny, but the nights were cool breezes moving through open windows.

Like a migrating bird, Samone began to feel her heart searching for a warm place to spend the winter.

The leaving of summer and the arrival of fall was a setup, but Samone, concerned with other things, didn't know that until after the fact.

5

Lunch. Samone and Jon did it often.

Meeting in the lobby, laughing, touching, coming together like conspirators. Eager to get outdoors, away from desks and ringing phones. Out into the fresh air, blue skies, city traffic.

Samone and Jon. On the streets. Eating, talking, walking, being together. Laughing, feeling good. Feeling special. Samone enjoyed these moments, her little rainbow.

Jonathon Everette. The most unwhite white man Samone had ever known. The only one she'd allowed into her world. She didn't tell anyone. Not her parents. Not Pat. Jon was her little secret.

Lunch. A needed warmth in her life, times where she felt special.

Dinner was a whole different matter.

"How about dinner?" he asked one day, minutes after biting into his hot dog.

"Dinner?" Samone said, choking on her soda.

His eyes pierced her, mischievous and conspiratorial. Those eyes, probing for a yes; giving her no way out.

"Straight after work," Jon offered, sweetening the pot. "Straight after," making it safe for her. She would not have to go home, change, and meet him somewhere. Samone would not have to fuss in her closet, decide on makeup or what perfume to wear. It would not be a real date, just a meal *after* work. She could eat and go straight home. The next day would be business as usual.

Dinner? her eyes asked.

"Yeah. After work. What do you say?"

What else could she say but, "Okay."

Samone hadn't thought of it as anything more than a change in her normal after-work routine. She was holding stubbornly to that thought when she met Jon in the lobby. He stood there, leaning against the wall, one hand in his pants pocket, legs crossed, waiting for her.

For me, she realized as she made her way to him.

In her haste or defiance, Samone hadn't even bothered to comb her hair or put on a touch of lipstick. It wasn't a date, she had decided minutes before locking her office, but all too late she realized it was. Jon took her hand, kissed her cheek, and moved her out into the streets.

The whole world seemed to slow down, and Samone took a moment to see Jon in a way she had never bothered to before. Lunch had always been about her. It was his turn now, his hour to shine.

The restaurant was quiet, dim, and intimate. The waiters spoke in soft, hushed tones, and the air was filled with the whisper of conversation and the tinkle of forks meeting china.

Sometime long after dinner had been eaten, Jon stopped talking. Samone found herself with a smile on her lips, leaning forward, watching him. Captivated with the sound of his voice, the sparkle in his eyes. His silence pulled her out of the moment, the joy of listening.

"What's wrong?" she asked.

He shook his head, pulling away from some important thought. "Nothing," he offered.

"You sure?"

"Yeah." He looked at his watch. "Better get you home." He signaled the waiter.

"You don't have to."

"It's okay."

"Really, Jon. I can get home by myself."

"You don't want me to?"

It had been so nice before, before talk of taking her home. Samone laughed and looked away. A smirk appearing as she looked back at him.

"No, I don't. But thanks for the offer."

He wouldn't argue the point. Stood up. "You ready?"

Samone searched for his smile. But he wasn't giving her one. *Oh, shit. What happened now? Did he really think 'cause he took me out and bought me a meal that he was gonna get some? Damn it to hell. . . . Fine, he's going to be greatly disappointed.*

As Jon paid with his American Express gold card, Samone let her eyes wander over the face that had been so full of charm just minutes ago. *I thought you were different. . . .*

Jon turned, tucking his wallet into his pants pocket. "You ready?" Samone nodded, not waiting for him as she headed toward the front door.

She spied an empty cab coming up the street and thought to hail it. But Jon's touch distracted her.

"There's something I have to tell you," he said.

"I'm listening." But she really wasn't. She filled her mind with other things to stave off the possibility that whatever he would say could affect her. That she would have to respond, decide; consider something. None of which she had been doing much of the evening.

So the humidity and the darkness relieved by street lamps and closed stores became her concern. Samone took in the dog that walked obediently on a leash in his master's hand and the comings and goings of patrons at a twenty-four-hour fruit stand.

She filled her mind with the steam rising from manhole covers and rap music that blasted from car stereos that passed them by.

"Can we walk?" he asked, uncertain. "I think better on my feet."

Whatever, Samone thought, walking with him, no direction in mind.

"I gotta apologize for this mood I'm in," Jon began.

"It's okay," Samone offered quickly.

"You're lying, but that's okay . . . wasn't going to say anything about this. I had decided that I would just keep quiet. Keep it to myself."

Samone shrugged, her eyes searching the traffic, in need of a cab. She really didn't want to know about any of the things Jon was saying now. It was his business, not hers.

"You have to know how I feel about you. . . ." Of course she did. But till this moment it had never been spoken. He stopped, looking at her. "I really like you. . . ." Paused. "A lot, Samone." And with that said, Jon started walking again.

Samone knew exactly what "a lot" meant. "A lot" was that place your heart went right before you actually loved someone. "A lot" was falling in love. Jon was falling in love with her.

There was no doubt that Samone liked him, enjoyed his company. No doubt that she felt good being around him. But there were limits to how deep their relationship could go, and love wasn't part of the equation.

Jon tried to hail her a cab, but without success. He lived only a few more blocks; did she want to come up and he'd try to call her one from there?

Sure, Samone said. Why the hell not.

Jon's apartment was done with modern furniture and lots of lithographs. Things in muted grays and charcoal. He had a thirty-inch color television set and a superior sound system, complete with a CD player, two tape decks, and an equalizer and receiver. The living room had skinny windows, but they went from floor to ceiling and the effect was breathtaking. The tall cactus in the corner immediately caught Samone's attention.

Samone's fingers were busy with its spindly needles when Jon told her it would be half an hour before the cab came.

"Can I get you something to drink?" he asked.

"Some cold water would be nice."

Everything in the room called out for her to come and touch. The glitter of the brass-framed pictures, the shine of the old world globe. Even the luster of the floor requested the presence of her toes. She was studying a Monet lithograph when he came back with her glass.

"How about some music?" Jon asked, moving to his stereo.

"It's not gonna be that white boy stuff, is it?"

"Huh?"

"You know. White boy music. Guns n' Roses, Led Zeppelin. The Rolling Stones?"

Jon popped out the cassette tape. "Actually, I was gonna play some Earl Klugh, but for being such a smart ass, I'm gonna put on what I call my golden oldies."

Samone took a seat, expecting the worst. Hard rock, no doubt. Or the syrupy psychedelic music from the early seventies. But what came out of his stereo was nothing she expected. The songs were as familiar to her as her last name. Carole King's "So Far Away," Elton John's "Your Song," Joni Mitchell's "Chinese Cafe," Phoebe Snow's "Poetry Man."

Samone sat up, protesting.

"Time out. Number one, you said 'golden oldies' and 'Chinese Cafe' ain't that old, and number two, you said they were your songs, which is a lie, 'cause all of them are mine." She looked at him a long time. "How did you know that?"

"I guess we got more in common than you thought."

"What'd you do, Jon, bug my living room for a month?"

Jon laughed, but Samone's face didn't move into anything close to a smile.

"I'm not laughing," she said, serious. "Did you?"

"I swear to God I didn't." He popped out the tape and gave it to her. "Look. It's so old the writing's come off."

Samone took it and examined it closely. The cassette did look as though it had spent too much time in the backseat of a car.

She gave it back. Moved on.

"Well, Phoebe Snow doesn't count. 'Cause even though she's Jewish, her voice is pure black."

"Phoebe? You got to be kidding me. I used to play her whenever I went cruising down the highway. Women loved it. Thought it was 'sensitive' of me to play it so much."

"You mean to tell me you used Phoebe Snow to get laid?"

"Oh, and you didn't?" he asked, incredulous.

The lie came easy. "No, I didn't." But of course she had. Michael Williams . . . she had been a sophomore in college. He was in his third year at Howard, home for the holidays.

Jon waved off her lie. "Yeah. Right."

She looked at him closely. "How do you know so much about me?"

"Your soul. I've seen your soul."

Samone snickered, amused by his nerve. "What, you're psychic?"

"I'll be anything you want me to be."

Samone laughed. *Niggas were niggas were niggas. . . .*

Jon pointed up the hall. "I'm gonna get out of these work clothes and hop into the shower. Anything else you want before I do?"

"No, I'm fine."

Samone sipped her water, slid out of her pumps, and laid her head back. She didn't want to close her eyes, but there was no distraction to keep them open. By the time Jon got back, she was dozing.

She came to with Jon's face close to hers. Could feel his breath, warm against her cheek. The closest they had ever been.

There was fear in her eyes, but even in her fear a part of her wanted the closeness. A part of her was curious, a part of her wanting to be held, kissed. To take it beyond the boundaries. To experience the love he was feeling for her.

In the moment, Samone wanted him as much as he wanted her. She wanted to have his arms around her, get skin to skin.

She saw the kiss coming and did nothing to stop him. Her head was dizzy, her heart beating fast. Her lips trembling, awaiting the feel of his lips on hers.

He moved his arms around her, felt her shiver, and held her closer to stop her trembling. The slope of her neck, satin soft; her hair tickling the backs of his hands.

Lips parting, his tongue sought hers. His longing, his want, pulling her deeper into him. This first kiss, new, gentle, and baby soft.

Kissing Jon. Taking her back; back to the days when all she did was kiss. To when kissing was the beginning, the middle, and the end. Where kissing was everything. No sex, just two lips making music.

Like now.

Wonderful. Magic. Kissing, pure and simple. He would kiss her all night if she let him. Would kiss her into morning, if that's what she wanted.

The attraction had been there for weeks, but Samone had refused to give it serious thought. Still, there'd been times when she could feel his heat, could feel his thoughts, the underlying current running between them.

It couldn't be like that for her, not with a white man, or so she'd thought. Here and now, she knew better. Knew she would take this moment as far as he would. Knew how far they'd go.

The phone began ringing.

So long, too long, Samone thought. Too long since someone's held me this way. Her last thought before Jon turned off the lights and turned up the music.

Morning.

Samone awoke in a panic. The familiarity of her bedroom did not soothe her. The sun streaming into her windows did not warm her. Samone lay there, eyes adrift, filled with dread.

What in the world have I done?

Jon hadn't attacked her. Had given her the opportunity to say no, but she hadn't. Samone did what she'd done because she had wanted to.

Last night she had lain in Jon's bed. Had lain in the darkness so willingly. The soft sheets that smelled of Final Touch tickling her spine. The body over and in her that was Jon. The smell of mojo sex heavy in the air, as though neither of them had made love in a long time, as though they had been waiting for each other forever.

You in me, Samone thought, unable to rise from her bed, all magic and rainbows and sailing high above everything. Music and stars and fields of daffodils. Falling, fast, far. Deep. . . . No black. No white. Just us. So good it scared me. . . .

Last night it had seemed like the most natural thing to do. Last night she'd had no doubt, no concerns; she'd wanted Jon. But in the bright light of morning she realized exactly what had happened. She had broken her own trust.

It would never be "one of those things." Would not be forgotten or dismissed. Jon was white. *And a Sista's always a Sista.* . . . What would Pat say? What would Pat think? Do? What in the world would her momma think? What would her friends say? Black folks she knew? Black folks she didn't know?

What in the world would they think of the Sista from Harlem now?

Sex changes everything. That was all Samone could consider as she arrived at work, moved through the glass doors of her office lobby, and joined the masses waiting by the elevator banks.

Her relationship with Jon had been fine before that night. *Before last night.* Samone closed her eyes on that thought.

Forget the fact that it had been the best sex she'd had since Max, the only sex since Max. It was still sex. Still sex with Jon. Still sex with a white man she had no intention of getting busy with. An excellent lover who had her calling his name as though she had loved him forever.

The elevator door opened, and Samone hurried inside.

She was a black woman and he was a white man. No way was she supposed to sleep with him and like it, *a lot.* . . .

She pressed the button for the fifth floor.

The elevator door opened and more people got on.

Somebody stepped on her toe. She said, "Ouch!" out loud.

Before last night, he was just this great flaky silly-ass white boy she hung with during work. Who'd call her interoffice and flirt with her all the time. And that was cool and sweet and fine, because Samone knew he'd never get the chance.

The elevator eased to her floor. She got a good hold on her pocketbook and readied herself to squeeze to the front.

And now here she was, sleeping with him. It didn't matter how funny he was or how cute he looked. All that mattered was she'd given it up to him willingly, and sex always changed everything.

Well, he better be cool with it, was all Samone knew, stepping off the elevator and running smack dab into him. She almost wet her pants.

"Jon?"

His face was full of torment. "I have to talk to you."

Samone looked away, nervous and embarrassed, filled with a funky shame that had no name.

"Now? Here?"

"It's important."

Samone closed her eyes, opened them.

"Come on, my office. But you got to make it quick. I got a nine-fifteen."

They moved swiftly down the hall.

"About last night . . ."

Samone held up her hand, hushing him. "Forget about it."

"It's not that simple, Samone."

She lit a cigarette and blew gray smoke. "How did I know that. . . . Look, Jon, we're friends, right? Something happened last night, it ain't the end of nobody's world. Certainly not mine . . . it's not that important."

His face was full of torment. "But it is."

"No, it's not." *And why you got to go deep into this? It ain't no big deal. We slept together. It was good. So the fuck what?*

"How can you say that?"

"Because it's the truth," she threw back, her voice rising.

"Is that how you feel?" Jon wanted to know.

"Yes." That was exactly how she was feeling this morning.

"Last night," he pleaded, as though it were the end of the world.

"What?"

He shook his head. Samone watched as he searched for words.

"It won't let me go."

Samone looked at him a very long time. She had never looked into those tiger eyes of his so long. Today they didn't sparkle, they consumed her. She moved past them.

"You *have* to," she demanded.

"Meet me for lunch," was his reply as he walked out the door.

* * *

Is it the pussy, Jon? Was it that good? This was what Samone wanted to ask, seated across from him in the faux chic fast-food eatery. Samone had listened to him talk for a long time. Jon told her all sorts of things about himself that she had never asked about.

He talked about Yvonne, the name coming up every other word. He talked openly and painfully about Yvonne's love for him and how that had not been enough to keep him. He talked about his weekend trips and the sweet love they used to make; how all they did now was argue.

And in the midst of all of this, Samone had come into his life.

Samone liked Jon, was all. She didn't love him and doubted she ever would, so there was nothing on her tongue that could make it better.

"Jon, we're friends. Do you understand? We do lunch, talk during work hours, and just buddy around. I just got out of a relationship and the last thing I'm looking for is another one. Ain't even about color." Which was a lie, but nobody was going to call her to the table on it.

Jon looked at his watch, spoke distractedly. "Look at the time. We better go."

As Samone stubbed out her cigarette and slid back her chair, she realized Jon hadn't heard a damn thing she'd just said.

"Did I tell you about what happened on my last flight to L.A.?"

"No, Jon. Tell me."

"Now you got to remember, I left straight from

work, no dinner or anything. I'm on the plane, and we hit some mean turbulence. Next thing I know, I got to throw up, but we're going through turbulence, so I'm not supposed to leave my seat, right? Well, I get up and go racing toward the toilet anyway. The stewardesses are yelling for me to come back, but I got to throw up. So I hurry to the bathroom and lock the door. Okay, my stomach's really starting to roll now. So just as I'm about to let go, the plane drops from beneath my feet and I miss the toilet by a mile. . . ."

This was the Jon that Samone liked best. The one that always had a funny story or a joke to tell. The one that was not asking for things she couldn't give.

"Hi. It's me. Max."

Samone never thought he'd call her office ever again. Shock held her tongue. She could not believe the Great and Powerful Max was calling her.

She looked at the applicant before her. "I can't talk now. Someone is in my office. I'll call you back."

"I'm at work."

"Yes, I know."

She didn't get the chance to call him back until an hour later. She found herself apologetic for the delay, even though he didn't deserve an apology.

"Sorry, been busy this afternoon," she told him.

"Been doing some thinking."

"Yeah." She was not going to make it easy for him.

"About us."

"And?"

"Can we meet, talk? After work? I'll be standing in my usual spot. Y'know, by the big white tree planter."

Samone felt relief wash over her. Her episode with Jon had scared her silly. The other night was an act of desperation as far as she was concerned, and she never wanted to be put in that situation again.

She needed the familiarity and stability of Max back in her life. There was no way she could tell him no.

"Okay."

The end of her workday could not come soon enough. Samone spent the last five minutes of it fixing her hair, putting on lipstick, checking her clothes in the office bathroom. At five o'clock she hurried to the elevators, nervous, anxious, and on fire.

She hurried across the lobby, the large glass doors her destination. Her whole body surged with love, giving her power, moving her on to the moment she would see him. She was on the street in seconds, her eyes eager for the sight of Max.

But the spot by the tree was empty.

Samone glanced at her watch and formulated reasons why he hadn't gotten there yet. For fifteen minutes she stood there, looking, shifting, smoking cigarettes till she was queasy. At seventeen minutes after five she reentered her office building and dialed his office. No answer.

Five-thirty she was still waiting. Samone held back

her fear and told her heart to be still. Then it began to rain, tiny sprinkles that found her uncovered head, misted against the natural fibers of her jacket.

He's coming.

Her hair limped and began clinging to the sides of her face. With care, Samone wiped water off her face, dimly wondering what picture she presented to pass-ersby.

He's coming. The rain, still a fine mist, clung to her lashes, dampened her brow, and gathered on her shoulders. Samone looked up the street, willing Max's arrival.

Come on, Max. Come on.

A fast wind erupted up the block, scattering news-papers, gum wrappers, and potato-chip bags. Samone turned her back against the gust, waiting for it to die down. But the wind had a surprise riding its coattails, and the heavens opened up.

Sheets of rain plummeted the sidewalks. Samone ran for the shelter of her office lobby, soaked by the time she reached it.

She stood by the window, shifting wet hair off her neck, wiping her face with chilled hands, her clothes limp and sodden. She waited, checking her watch, dripping wet for what seemed an eternity.

She looked at her watch one final time—five thirty-eight—and knew.

Max was not coming.

Samone closed her apartment door, slipped out of her shoes, and went to the phone. Dialed Max and got no answer.

She got out of her wet things, put on her terry-cloth robe, and tried him again. No answer. Samone moved to the kitchen, put the kettle on for tea, and tried Max again. Still no answer.

Her tea was steeping when she tried him a fourth time. Quarter to seven, where was he? Something terrible must have happened. Maybe he'd been mugged and was lying bleeding in the streets somewhere. Maybe he'd got caught up and tried to phone her while she was waiting. Maybe something had happened to his father and he'd had to rush to the Bronx.

Or maybe . . .

Samone turned away from that thought.

She dialed Pat, her tale rushing out the moment Pat picked up. A good friend, Pat at least let her finish before she told her, "He's in the living room having a beer with Ray."

"What? He was supposed to meet me."

"I know, Sam. But he's a little mixed up."

"A little? I waited forty-five minutes for his ass, in the fucking rain!" The reality, the stupidity, the needy hungry desperation, came to her like a bolt of lightning. She had not thought about it on the cab ride home. Had not thought about it as she'd changed wet clothes, as she'd tossed her ruined suede shoes into the garbage. As she'd made tea and tried to reach him by phone.

Samone had not considered it as she'd made up scenarios as to why he had not come. But now that she knew, she was livid.

"Look, I know you're upset and he's upset that he

couldn't make it. But look, Samone. Just trust me on this. Max is at a vulnerable point in his life, okay? We got to do this right.''

''We? What we?'' she wanted to know. ''What the fuck is this we, Pat? . . . I don't believe you. You're always taking up for him. What about me? I was the one waiting. I thought you were my friend.''

''Don't even try that, Samone. I'm both your friends. I just want what's best for you.''

Samone nearly choked on her words, her mouth barely able to keep up with all she wanted to say. ''Oh, and him over there making me wait is best for me? He could have at least called, Pat.''

''Look, Samone. I'm not gonna tell you again. You want Max? Then you just lay low. You hear me? Just lay low. . . . I gotta go. Call you later.''

But she didn't. And neither did Max.

6

"You treating today? I'm low on cash."

Samone heard Jon ask but didn't answer; her mood was blue.

"Hello? Earth to Samone."

"What!"

"Jumpy, aren't we."

"Oh, just shut up, Jon. Just shut the hell up." There. She'd said it. Did she mean it? Yes. Was she sorry? Only a tiny bit. Samone had other concerns, and the least of them was Jon. Her personal life was shit, and he'd just have to understand that without her explaining a damn thing.

"Fine. I'll shut up."

Samone nodded, a bewildered afterthought caught in the midst of her dilemma.

It's this waiting. I'm doing what Pat said to do.

I'm waiting. Laying low. But the phone has not rung once in all this waiting. Max didn't even call to apologize about not meeting me. But I'm supposed to be cool. How long does Pat think this coolness can last?

"How about Central Park and some franks," Jon proposed. A quick cheap meal, she would be out six bucks, the most. He was about to ask again when he realized that lunch was the least of her concerns. He had never seen her look so engrossed.

"What's wrong, Samone?"

"Nothing. . . . Can we walk a little faster? We only got an hour."

Jon pressed her. "Not till you tell me what's wrong."

"I said nothing." *Nothing you need to know. . . .* Wasn't nobody's business but hers and Max's. If she didn't want to tell it, then she didn't have to.

Jon stopped, but Samone kept walking. She was a few yards ahead when she realized it. She saw him behind her and knew he was waiting for an explanation. Her blood boiled. The last thing she needed was some crap from him today.

"You coming or what," Samone wanted to know, prepared to go on without him.

Jon's voice became full of all sorts of things: concern, compassion, empathetic hurt. "Not until you tell me."

But Samone wasn't bending. She wasn't telling him nothing about anything. He could stand there all

damn day, looking hurt over shit he knew nothing
about; it didn't move her . . . much.

"Drop it, Jon," she warned.

Jon wasn't backing down. "I'm not moving till you
tell me what's going on."

*Going on? Like my worries has something to do
with you? Don't flatter yourself.* Samone looked at
him. Saw a man. A white one at that. *A white man
who I've given my booty to. . . .*

"Suit yourself," Samone decided, heading the
straight line up Seventh Avenue that would take her
to Central Park. Leaving Jon behind was the least of
her worries.

*You wait. But what are you waiting for? Marriage?
A ring? For Max to confess his undying love to you?
What exactly do you believe is at the other side of his
rainbow? A pot of gold or a trunk full of junk?*

*You been waiting a week, okay? And the brother
hasn't dropped a single dime your way. What are you
waiting for, Samone?*

Answers.

She made a left at Fifty-ninth Street. Unannounced,
she would go in search of answers, and damn it to
hell, Maxwell Aaron Scutter was going to tell her
something.

"Is he in?" Some things were automatic. Like the
hairs rising on the back of Samone's neck as Angela
turned away from her computer and looked up at her.

Angela was Max's secretary.

Angela had Samone's home address in her Rolodex. On the November 16 page of her desk calendar, for the past four years, Angela had written the words "Samone's birthday tomorrow" in red letters, just in case it slipped Max's mind.

Angela was thirty-something and Italian. Angela was competent and sexy, and they both knew it. This woman, yet to be married, had worked for Max longer than Samone had slept with him.

"Oh, Samone . . . hold on, let me buzz him."

Samone raised her hand. "No . . . it's a surprise, if that's okay."

"Sure. Go on in. He's having lunch."

"Thanks." She turned and paused before the heavy oak door. Watched her hand rise and settle on the brass sculptured knob. Gripped it and gave it a gentle twist. Paused another second before she eased the door open, her heart beating double time.

Max, having just swallowed the last of the deli potato salad, turned to dump the plastic container into the paper bag when he heard the door open. He took his feet off his desk and unconsciously straightened his tie. His face registered surprise seeing Samone standing there.

"Samone?"

"I tried waiting, Max. Tried to wait for you to call me. But you didn't. And I couldn't go another day without something."

Max's arms moved about him, suggesting the putty-colored lateral files and the oak desk. The solid brass banker's lamp, financial journals, and New York

State banking reports. His motion implied expensive lithographs by famous dead painters.

"Here?"

"It was the only place I knew I could find you."
I don't want to be here, either, but you gave me no choice.

"Not here, baby. Never here." Samone had known that from the minute she had decided it would have to be here.

"So what are you saying?" she managed, holding his face steady, the urge to blink and look away heavy in her sadness.

What am I saying? . . . Max had worked hard to become the director of mortgage. He'd studied hard in school, read *The New York Times, The Wall Street Journal,* and *Crain's New York Business* every time they hit the newsstand. Max had studied the young white male yuppies on Wall Street until he'd gotten the look down to such a science, it was as if he had invented the style himself.

He'd worked his way from a teller to a member services representative, biting down on the fact that he had a bachelor's in liberal arts. And when it became apparent that four years of college would not take him off the banking floor, he'd taken courses at Columbia University in financial management and kept on applying for positions in the Mortgage Department on the third floor, until they'd cried uncle and given in.

He'd started as a mortgage representative and put in late hours. He was always professional, on time, and polite. The black secretarial pool labeled him "Uncle Tom," but he knew what he had to do and did it.

Working full-time and going to Columbia part-time, Max had gotten his MBA in two years and the corporation had made him assistant director of mortgage. When the manager moved on to a better job, Max, having been politically correct from the beginning, was given the position.

While after work you might catch him hanging with his homeboys, slapping five and talking loud, at work he was as straight as the stays in the collar of his business shirts.

That's the way Max played it. And he was recalling all of this as he looked at Samone standing in front of him.

"Samone, you know my personal life and my professional life don't ever get together. They are separate. The last thing I would do, even for you, is talk 'love shop' here.

"You know they are always looking for a reason to get me out of here. You know that there's a whole line of white Anglo-Saxon Japanese Chinese Protestant Catholic Jewish atheists waiting in line for my position. And while they may buy me a beer and talk about the Knicks, to them I'm just a black boy who got lucky. And luck didn't have shit to do with it. This is not the time or the place, okay?"

Samone studied him. A perfect mortgage manager, complete with neatly combed hair and clothes sharp as a tack. Nowhere did she see the man who could say how much he loved her with just a smile.

She knew his struggle. Didn't need reminding about what it had taken him to get here. What she needed was for him to give her what he had promised over a week ago.

"Then when, Max?" Samone knew the bell was about to ring to tell her that her time was up or maybe that she had ten seconds to get to the core. "You promised me a week ago."

"Soon, baby." His eyes were pleading, but Samone refused the signal.

"How soon is *soon*, Max?"

His intercom buzzed and he picked up, turning his back to her. Speaking in low, important tones, he put the call on hold; turned back to her, his anger a slow burn.

"I have a call."

"Is that supposed to be my cue?" Samone was walking around land mines now, and she knew it. But she was feeling reckless and would not walk away without something from him.

Max swallowed, his palm damp as it clutched the phone. "Business is business, Samone."

For a second, Samone did not respond. Considered the person before her. Could see the little red light flashing, indicating that like herself, somebody else was on hold. Blinked back tears when she realized that it was this other person who would get his immediate attention.

Her hand played and lost, Samone knew it was time to go.

"I'm going, Max . . . since it's the wrong place and time and all."

Max sighed, pushed the extension, and spoke briefly. He hung up and moved toward her.

Her heart melted in his arrival.

This is all I want. I want to know that I matter, no matter where or how. I want to know that nothing will keep you from me, not even your job.

Samone looked away as he reached for her; her whole body swallowed in his embrace. She closed her eyes, heard his heart beating, and she knew she was alive again.

Max looked around his office, his eyes settling on reprint paintings by the Old Masters long dead; people he never knew, never talked to, never touched. Realized there wasn't a single picture of Samone anywhere and closed his eyes to the sacrifices made.

The plan was that he would try to meet her at her job about five, but he had called and told her he was running late and that he would meet her at her place.

He mentioned that he was hungry and maybe she might want to make him something so that he wouldn't have to stop on the way. He praised her baked fish and said he had a taste for broccoli with cheese sauce. Samone took the hint.

She stopped at the fish store and bought kingfish steaks. Got a head of broccoli, a lemon, some russet potatoes, and a half pound of American cheese.

Loaded down with groceries, Samone hummed a

happy melody as she entered her apartment and dumped the bags by the kitchen table.

She made her bed, took a quick shower, and wrapped up in her favorite peach bath sheet. She turned on the jazz station, poured a glass of wine, and started cooking. She had just placed the cheese over the steamed broccoli when her intercom buzzed.

"Who?"

"Me, baby."

And in that nothing beat a failure but a try, Samone allowed hope in. Felt it dance about her as she waited for the sound of the elevator, the echo of his leather soles on the hard polished hallway floor, and the *bing! bong!* of her doorbell.

Life always gave you choices, Max considered as Samone closed the door behind her and smiled, arms extended.

With a flick of his wrist, he could undo that peach towel. He could embrace her and run his fingers across her flesh. He could coax her into another shower and take her up against the ceramic bathroom tiles.

He could hold her all night and never talk. But that wasn't why he was here, so he kissed her lips lightly, undid his tie, and asked, as if he had never been gone, "Dinner ready? I'm starved."

Samone tried to decipher his brush-off. Maybe in the midst of things Max had missed her signal. He wasn't supposed to eat now, he was supposed to relieve her of her towel and run his tongue over her breasts and belly. He was supposed to fall to his knees in front of her and burrow his lips into the hairs below her belly. He was supposed to moan and sigh and tell her how much he had missed it. Not peck her cheek and head toward her kitchen as though his name were on the lease.

She went and put something on.

When she came back, he had her plate ready. A tall glass of Coca-Cola fizzed. Her knife and fork was on a folded paper towel. A small envelope rested beneath the edge of the plate.

She saw the envelope and purposely ignored it. Her ego had been burned and was still smoking in the aftermath of his rejection. Max, hard between her thighs, was what she had wanted, and nothing in that card would come close.

She ate without interest and refused to look at him. Afterward Max cleared the table. Samone, hugging her muteness like an old friend, went to the living room to have a smoke. Max remained behind and did the dishes.

For a long time she listened to the sounds of running water and silverware jangling together. She heard a cabinet door open and knew he was going to scrub the bottom of her aluminum pot with Brillo. He'd dry all the dishes and put them away. The pots would be left wet and clean on top of her stove.

"That's the way my momma taught me," he had told her a long time ago.

"Don't do this."

So intent was her funk that Samone had not seen

him standing there. She jumped, and soda sloshed everywhere.

"Shit," she said to nobody, especially not Max. Her mind was already in the kitchen, snatching paper towels off the roll, as she checked herself for wet spots.

Knowing the extent of her anger, Max let her pass and got out of her way as she returned. Stood by as she began wiping the couch and the front of her night-shirt. Didn't blink as she glared at him, as if it had all been his fault and she was waiting for him to say it. Allowed his mouth to move a fraction of an inch toward a smile as she said, "Shit," smirked, and went to throw the damp paper towels in the garbage.

In her absence, he put Patti LaBelle on the stereo.

"You want to hear that?" Samone asked, listening to the first strands of "Come What May."

"Yeah. Don't you? You love this song."

In another time and space she had, but not now. There were too many emotions in that song that belonged to her privately; things she would never share.

"A lot of things I love; that doesn't mean I necessarily want it at this moment."

Obliging, Max lifted the needle off the record, carefully slid the album off the turntable. And with the same carefulness, he put the vinyl back into its jacket. He faced her, hands up.

"I surrender."

"What?"

"I said I surrender."

"To what?"

"Whatever this war is about. I surrender."

War? Was there a war going on? Samone shook her head, her face confused. What in the world was he talking about? Then it dawned on her. She sighed and looked away.

"This ain't no war, Max."

"Most certainly is. And I'm battle shocked and wounded. So I'm giving up." He meant it.

"Fine, there was a war, you surrendered. Fine."

Max lost his cool, his patience; the art of forgiveness.

"I don't understand you, Samone. I'm here. Standing right here, ready to do whatever is necessary to get us back together, and you are over there like I'm the last fucking person you want to see."

Maybe you are. . . . The words almost escaped, but she clamped down hard and swallowed. She realized he was right and let her anger go.

"I'm sorry," she said.

Max gave her a rueful smile, looking over his shoulder. "Go to the kitchen. I believe there's an envelope waiting with your name on it."

Samone went.

On the front of the card were two brown hands entwined; inside, in the penmanship she had always loved, were three words: I love you.

Samone slid to the floor and cried. Was still there when Max walked in. He got down on the floor and held her. A long time.

"We can do this, Samone."

"You sure, Max? Are you sure?" Because she

wasn't, not at all. All she was certain of was that he had left her months ago in need of space. That some gap-toothed fat woman had snatched him away from her. That he had been gone a long time and now was back, talking about second chances. Samone had no guarantees about tomorrow.

"Sure as sure can be." His eyes danced into hers, his finger moving over the bridge of her nose. "You got such a cute nose."

She became aware of his heat, which rose up like a volcano, and his breath, spicy and warm. Samone felt his teeth nibbling at the sensitive spot on her neck, and she moaned.

She lay back against the cool black-and-white kitchen tiles. Closed her eyes and parted her thighs. Felt his warm, wet tongue caress her calf, play hop-scotch: soft kisses here, soft kisses there.

She shivered.

Her nipples hardened beneath the cotton of her nightshirt. Her spine arched without thought.

Then the heat of him was gone. Free air moved along her cheek, her neck, her thighs. Samone opened her eyes and saw him standing, hand extended toward her.

"Not here," he said.

Samone shook her head gently. "Yes, right here."

"No, not here."

Her eyes were on fire. "Yes." She needed him now, that very second, could not waste time going down the hall to her bed. She was desperate for him and reached for his belt buckle. Max pulled away. But

Samone held on, her fingers fast upon his zipper.

She didn't know herself but did not care.

Samone forced his pants to his knees, and Max tumbled, catching the edge of the counter with his shoulder.

His hand rubbed his wounded shoulder. "Damn it, Samone"—he looked down at her as if she had gone insane—"what is wrong with you?"

She struggled for an answer, her eyes wild and confused. "I've missed you."

"I miss you, too. But I haven't had a shower since morning, and I'll be damned if I'll make love on a cold, hard-ass floor"—his demeanor softened—"when there's a nice warm soft bed. . . ." He took her by the hand. "Come on."

But her desire was gone by the time Max emerged from the bathroom. Not even the sight of him naked moved her heart much. Something had died there on the kitchen floor, something sanctimonious and absolute.

Samone rolled away from him as he got into bed.

"I'm sorry, babe," he offered, sensing her mood.

"It's not enough, Max, not anymore."

"What, 'cause I didn't want to make love on the kitchen floor?"

"No, Max."

"Then what, baby, what?" He sucked her neck gently, and despite herself, her body responded.

"What?" Max asked again, his big warm fingers moving over her belly.

"Nothing." But Samone knew exactly what it was.

7

The newscasters had been talking about heavy rains hitting New York since last Thursday. But Friday had been as warm and dry as Thursday, and the weekend was no different. After a while, people stopped paying the weatherman much mind, relying on their bedroom window for the daily forecast.

Having spent the entire weekend at Max's, Samone awoke to the rainy Monday with Max sipping coffee and already dressed. It was so dark outside that the streetlights were still on. Samone could not believe it when he said it was a quarter after seven.

"It's so dark," she mumbled, the need for sleep as thick as the comforter she huddled under.

"Yeah. It's the rain."

Samone peeked at the clock for verification. The blood red digits glowed feral and exact: 7:15. She knew the only place she would be going this particular morning was back to sleep. Her concern for the moment was waking up at the right time to call in sick.

If she called work before 9:00, she'd get a manager; if she called at exactly 9:01, she'd get Merissa. Better to tell lies to the subordinates than your peers. She sat up and reached for Max's alarm.

Max straightened his tie, moving to his closet to find his Totes. "Not going in?"

"No . . . are you?" Samone had caught the condemnation in his voice. He was accusing her of something, and she knew exactly what it was. A sore point between them, it was an issue they avoided. The way Samone saw it, Max was a "house nigga" and only too happy to be one. She, on the other hand, felt her only obligations in life were to stay black and die. Work was something you did out of necessity, not choice. You went to work to put food in your belly and a roof over your head. Beyond a paycheck, there was little else work was supposed to be.

Samone watched Max half-bent into his closet, searching intently for his rubber Totes. *It's his whole life.* Monday through Friday, eight A.M. to five P.M., Max answered to one god, and its name was Work.

He kissed her. "Gotta run. I'll call you later."

"I should be gone about noon," Samone offered, glad he was finally leaving.

"There's bagels and cream cheese in the fridge." And then the front door was closing.

Samone did not envy him.

8

It was Samone's thirty-fifth birthday, but she was no closer to getting married now than she had been last year. The truth overwhelmed her.

Samone opened the box again, making sure her eyes hadn't been playing tricks. Saw the gold earrings and swallowed the need to cry.

"You don't like them," Max said, distressed.

"No, it's not that I don't like them. . . ." She fought tears.

"Then what's wrong?"

"Nothing . . . thanks," she managed, not looking at him.

"How about some champagne now?"

"Sure." Samone got off the couch and went to get glasses. How could he think a pair of earrings could ever mean more to her than a ring? Thirty-five years old. She had been seeing Max since she was thirty-one. When in the hell were they supposed to get married, when she was forty?

Samone reached into her cabinet, grabbing the tulip goblets.

Of course she'd have to keep quiet about her disappointment, couldn't let him know. If she told him, they'd end up arguing for sure.

It *was* her birthday.

Samone closed the cabinet door, resisting the urge to slam it. Was she supposed to wait forever, is that what he thought?

She headed back to the living room, caring less about the champagne. She handed him the glasses. He filled both, gave her one, and raised his own.

"To you, babe."

Samone nodded, unable to find the muscles to smile.

"*Salute,*" he said, sipping in her direction. "I know something's up. What? You wanted Kahlúa instead of champagne?"

When Samone wouldn't respond, Max turned away. She could tell by the way his shoulders were hunching that her secret was out. The last thing she needed was his anger, which was exactly what she got.

He faced her, at wits' end. "Nothing I do seems to be right, does it."

"Max, I—"

But he didn't want to hear a thing she had to say. "I bought you the best damn pair of earrings in Littmons . . . got a limo to pick you up from work . . . a dozen yellow roses special delivery. Take you to dinner and bring you home, give you your gift, and suddenly it's all wrong.'' He looked at her, his anger moving fast into hurt. His voice, a hoarse whisper.

''I don't get you.'' He shook his head, dazed and confused. ''What did I do wrong? Planned everything just so it'd be perfect. Still wasn't right.'' He looked at her, hurt. ''It was your birthday, babe . . . your birthday. The most important day in your life, and I still didn't get it right.''

Max stopped talking, and the silence became worse than his fury. He stared at her, trying to understand what it was she had needed. Trying to understand how the best of his plans had not been enough. Max stared till he realized it was the same old story. Samone wanted a ring.

He shook his head, disgusted and wearied. After all this time, she still didn't get it. He wasn't going to ask her to marry him until he was ready. Didn't she know that by now?

He sighed, full of defeat. Looked at her once more, needing her to accept the love he was able to give. Samone knew he was hurting, that she had hurt him, but she was hurting, too, and there was no way she could change it or make it easier for either of them. She could not hide her disappointment or wish away her wants. She wanted a ring, not some damn earrings.

Max got his coat and left without another word. It

was the second time he had walked out on her.

Samone wondered if there would be a third.

Samone could have told Jon no. Could have told him that her birthday had been a disaster and she didn't want to indulge it any further. But that would mean telling the business between her and Max, and she wasn't willing to do that. So when Jon called and said he was coming down with her belated birthday gift, she said okay.

"What is it?" she asked, taking the gold-wrapped gift.

"It's a box."

Samone had no patience. "What is it, Jon?"

"A birthday gift. You gonna open it or not? I can't stay long."

Samone eyed him and handed it back. "I can't take it."

"Why not?"

"I can't."

"Sure you can."

"It's not right."

" 'Course it is. Here. Open it."

It dawned on her that if Jon wanted to give it—no strings attached—then she had the right to accept it. And if it turned out to be something she couldn't use, she'd give it back.

Samone attacked the pretty paper in a frenzy, shreds of gold littering her desk. Her mouth fell open as she looked at the Mickey Mouse watch with the gold band and diamond where the number 12 was supposed to be.

"Oh, Jon, it's gorgeous."

"You like it?"

"Like it? I love it. Oh, but I can't take this . . . it must have cost a fortune."

"It's only a Mickey Mouse watch."

"Only? Jon, it's gold and has a diamond. It couldn't be cheap." She was looking at him, searching his face for a sign of how he had come to know her so well.

"Well, the diamond's real. The gold's not. After a few wears, your arm falls off."

Fourteen karat or gold plated, it didn't matter. It was beautiful and different, something that she would have never thought to buy for herself.

"You are something, you know that? You are really something," she told him.

Jon leaned over and kissed her lips lightly. "Happy birthday."

She looked up at him with soft eyes. "Thank you," she offered, her voice tender. Her gratitude, a fragile whisper. Her eyes glistening with a tender fire.

Thirty-five years old. As Samone made her way across the street, Pat saw her best friend was still looking good.

"Late as usual," Pat began, kissing her cheek.

"Fuck you. . . . Where you taking me?"

"McDonald's, where else?" Which was typical Pat. She did not believe in fancy restaurants. Could not stand to pay more than four bucks for any meal. McDonald's was Pat's favorite place to eat, and even though it was her best friend's birthday gift, she wasn't about to change now.

Pat's eyes danced, eager for the details. "So . . . how was it?"

"Oh, Pat, you ain't gonna believe this shit."

"What happened?"

"Let me put it to you this way: The man I had hoped to get a diamond from didn't give me one. And the man I didn't expect shit from, did."

"What?"

"Come on. I got a whole truckload to dump on you."

Samone had a Big Mac, a large fries, and a strawberry shake. Was slurping in the last bit when she got to the part about Jon and the watch.

"That watch is bad, Samone."

"Don't I know it."

"You sure you ain't giving this white boy no booty?"

"I take the Fifth," Samone offered, deciding to let go of her secret.

"I knew it! Damn. A fucking white boy. . . . Well, was he any good?"

"None of your damn business."

"Musta been. You still talking to him."

"You'll never know."

"So you talk to Max?"

"No. What could I possibly say?"

"Anything it'll take."

"I hurt him, Pat. I hurt him real bad."

"Yeah, but you were expecting a ring. After four years, I guess I would, too."

"I hear a 'but' in there."

"No 'but.' You been with him a long time. You have a right to be disappointed."

"Thank God. I thought it was just me."

"Look, Samone. Max is my friend, but so are you. About time he did the right thing."

"You know something I don't?"

"I know that this burger gonna have me going to the bathroom all night."

"Oh, that's funny. Real funny."

Pat flipped her wrist. "Look at the time. I gotta get going."

"Well, thanks for the birthday meal, no matter how cheap or late."

Pat looked at her friend. She smiled carefully, knowing she wasn't God, that she didn't have foresight into the future. That Samone trusted her with many things.

"Samone, don't take your disappointment as the end. By now you know it ain't over till it's over."

"Pat, I—"

"Just listen, okay? You hurt his feelings; he's hurt yours. It ain't the first time, and it probably won't be the last. This is real life; what makes us grown. And if Max is what you want, then you have to follow through."

"He's not talking to me."

"How do you know?"

"I don't."

"Maybe it's time you find out. Now, come on. I gotta get that express before it starts running local."

There was a part of Max that was still furious; a part of him refusing to give up his hurt and was holding stubbornly to her being insensitive and ungrateful.

Samone had never been straightforward about wanting an engagement ring. She had hinted and joked about it, but she'd never come straight out and said she wanted to get married. She knew Max well enough to know that he wouldn't ask until he was ready. And he wasn't ready.

Still, there was the other part of him that welcomed the sound of her voice on the phone.

"Max? It's me."

"Hi."

"I was wrong," she began, "and I want to apologize. I acted totally ungrateful, and I am grateful."

"You wanted an engagement ring."

"Guess I did."

"But you know it's not like that. Not now."

"If it was ever like that at all. . . . Look, Max. This is old news. I been wanting a ring for the past two and a half years. But I can't make you do something you don't want to do."

"It's not what I want right now."

"Yeah, so I've heard. . . . Hey, look, in comparison to some, my birthday was wonderful. The more I think about it, the more I know how much you care for me."

"I do love you."

"Yeah, Max. I know that." But something in her had died.

"So what else did you get for your birthday?"

"Gift certificate from my folks, a six-dollar meal from Pat, and a Mickey Mouse watch."

"Mickey Mouse? From who?"

"My friend at work."

"Mickey Mouse? Well, that's different."

Yes, Samone thought, he certainly is.

"I'll be over tomorrow night."

"Can't wait," she told him.

9

Max lay in the dark, staring at the ceiling. Beside him, Samone slept the sleep of the dead. Max was thinking hard, trying to tell himself that he was wrong. That Samone knew her body better than he did. Knew the safe times.

Samone looked different these days. Felt different, too. Max had made love to her too often not to notice the change. And she definitely *felt* different.

She was late this month. And tired most of the time.

Max gazed at her in the darkness. Head back, mouth open. Snoring hard.

Max remembered the night it probably happened. There had been no trip to the bathroom, her normal thing to do.

Heat of the moment.

Max closed his eyes.

His friends would ask him, "Where was the condom, man?" But Max didn't use condoms with Samone. He didn't like them, and Samone had never asked him to. Now he wished he had.

No . . . Samone's too smart. No ring, no baby, so she couldn't be. Besides, she'd done it before, not getting up to put in her diaphragm, and *nothing happened, right? She knows her body.* Nothing ever happened before.

But Max wasn't so sure about this time.

Lureen Scutter eased the candied yams out of her oven, hoisting the heavy pan onto the top of her stove. She had been in the kitchen most of the day, preparing Christmas dinner.

"Sweetheart, pass me that server."

"This one?" Samone asked, at the ready in Max's mother's kitchen.

"Yeah, that'll be just fine."

Lureen Scutter paused, lifting a silver curl from her forehead. "How you doing, sweetheart? You been doing okay?" Samone hadn't looked too good. Dark circles peeking beneath her makeup, her eyes raw looking, as though she were about to cry.

Samone looked away, embarrassed by the concern. Seemed Lureen Scutter cared for her more than her son ever would. Unconsciously she rubbed the joint of her third finger. There was nothing in its way.

"I've been okay, Mrs. Scutter."

Lureen looked at Samone once more, not staring

too long. That left hand was still bare. Was the first place she had looked when Max and Samone arrived at her front door. Max was foolish. Didn't realize the treasure he had in Samone. This was their fifth Christmas. All you had to do was look at Samone and you knew there wouldn't be too many more.

"Well, I'm glad. . . . Take these rolls to the table, will you, sweetheart? The turkey'll be ready in a minute."

Samone loved Mrs. Scutter's homemade yeast rolls, but today she had no appetite. This morning she had been feeling nauseated.

Not confirmed, but Samone knew. She had planned on telling Max right after she opened her Christmas present, but the gold bracelet he'd given didn't warrant her telling.

It would have been okay, having a baby so soon after the wedding. Her mother would understand; so would Max's. Mrs. Scutter would be overjoyed.

Samone placed the rolls on the table.

Six settings were empty, awaiting the Christmas feast: turkey, roast beef, sweet potatoes, two kinds of gravy, peas and carrots, and coconut cake for dessert. Max, his father, his sister, and his sister's friend were all in front, watching television. Samone's place at holiday time was always in the kitchen with Mrs. Scutter.

Samone L. Scutter. Hard on the tongue, but it suited her just fine.

She looked down at her hand. The half-inch gold

bracelet shimmered but brought her no joy. *I hope I'm not. I swear to God I hope I'm not.*

"Sweetheart?"

"Yes, Mrs. Scutter." "Momma" was so much easier. That's what Max called her, what Lureen herself had tried to get Samone to do. But Samone couldn't do that until she was a Scutter, too.

"Come and get the cranberry sauce and the gravy."

"Yes, ma'am."

A shadow fell across the table, stealing the sparkle from the Waterford crystal goblets and the glimmer from the gold-rim dinner plates.

"Dinner ready yet? I'm starving."

Samone looked up. Saw Max standing there. Her wide eyes showed all her fear, all her sorrow. She longed to look away, to be private with this pain, but she couldn't. It was a long time before the words came.

"Your mother said the turkey's almost done."

Max looked away from her, and it made her want to cry. Made her turn away, seeking the warmth of the kitchen.

"You okay, sweetheart?" Mrs. Scutter asked again as Samone moved to the counter, her mind determined not to drop the bowl of jellied cranberries or spill the contents of the gravy bowl.

The lie came quickly. "I'm fine."

No, she would never tell Max. Do what she'd have to do and not say a word.

*   *   *

You rush.

Buying gifts. Wrapping presents. Putting up Christmas trees and decorating windows. You race across town, state, country, doing that "holiday got to eat dinner with the folks and friends" shuffle. You spend so much time racing that you need another holiday just from the holiday. Samone yawned, tired and sleepy. Wasn't no place she'd rather be than home in her bed.

She tried to fluff up. She was meeting Jon for lunch.

The elevator eased to a gentle stop. Jon was at his usual place. Samone smiled hard. Her greeting, "Hi," arrived before she did. Smiled harder as he looked her over close. *He knows something.* It was in the frown that moved across his face right before he spoke.

"Thank you for gracing me with your presence . . . long time no see."

Samone nodded her head in agreement. "I know. How was Christmas? I have your gift."

"Okay," Jon answered. "And yours?" The first thing he had done was check her hand. No ring. He was very glad about that.

"It was okay. . . . Jon, I want to ask you something."

"Go ahead."

"Not here. Let's go to Minnie's. We can sit there."

"Minnie's it is."

Most people believed the place was called Minnie's because it was so tiny. The property had been divided straight down the middle, offering up two stores in a space meant for one. But Minnie's was named after its owner, one Minifred Wilkins.

Minnie's was clean, the help was friendly, and the food was prepared with that real down-home flavor. Minnie's didn't serve quiche, sushi, or pasta, unless you counted the macaroni and cheese. The water came from a filtered tap, and the only alcohol they had was Miller beer.

If you ordered beef, you got more than three thin slices sharing space with a couple of string beans. Minnie's served up real food for people who took eating seriously.

With three tables, one booth, and a four-stool counter, Minnie's was always full of people.

For the first time ever, Samone and Jon got the booth.

Samone handed over the brightly wrapped box. "First things first. Your gift."

Jon shook it. "What is it? Feels like a box of air."

"Just open it, all right?" Samone sipped her water, not the least bit hungry. She watched Jon take the mouse out of the box.

"A stuffed animal?" He looked confused.

"Don't you get it?" Samone asked.

"Get what?"

"Mickey Mouse. I got you a Mickey Mouse doll."

Jon shrugged. "I see that."

"And?" She was impatient now.

"And? Well, it's black and white and red."

"No, Jon. Think."

"Mickey Mouse. Disneyland? California?. . . . Oh! I get it. Because I'm from California and Mickey's from California."

Samone looked at him. "No," she said softly, "Mickey Mouse as in the watch you gave me." Everything was wrong, and nothing she planned was coming out right. She felt overwhelmed. She knew she was going to cry; the tears long overdue. Didn't take much to release them.

"Hey, Samone"—Jon plucked a napkin from the holder—"it's okay. I love it. Really." When she made no effort, he reached over and dabbed her cheek. A tear escaped his paper chase, sliding softly down her cheek.

She shook her head. "No, Jon. It's not all right."

"I didn't mean to upset you, I was joking. I got it right away. Mickey Mouse . . . the watch."

Samone smiled wistfully, left brow raised, eyes averted. "No, it's not the gift."

"Then what is it?"

She was studying him now, studying him real hard. Trying to read all that lurked behind his eyes. Trying to measure the depth of his concern.

"Are we friends?"

"Of course. You know how I feel about you."

"Good friends?"

"As far as I'm concerned."

"Can you keep a secret? Can you listen and not say anything?"

"Sure."

Samone blinked. "Tomorrow, at nine in the morning . . .'' She paused, a new rush of sadness washing over her. ''I'm going to have''—she looked up at him, her eyes a brush fire: Jon, the only person she would tell—''an abortion.''

It was the last thing he had expected her to say. For a moment he was speechless.

''Is someone going with you?''

Those words touched her heart. Jon didn't ask why, how come, or ''Don't''; things that Max, Pat, or her mother would have. He knew the choice was hers and hers alone.

It felt good to tell it, to speak it out loud. Get the burden off her shoulders. And he was being so good about it, too. Respecting whatever she felt she needed.

''No. Nobody else knows.''

His next question was no surprise. Anyone would ask. Would be the first thing they would. ''Not even Max?''

''I didn't tell him.''

''Why not?''

Samone couldn't answer. Her reasons were foggy and without explanation. In another time and space, she decided. In another time and space, I will ask myself that question, even if I already know the answer.

Jon sat back. Looked away, looked back at her. He wondered if he was the only person Samone could tell. Where were the people who were supposed to love her? Without thought, he leaned forward, gathering her hands into his own.

''I'll come with you, if you want.''

''Don't be silly. I can do it alone.''

His touch was insistent. "Samone, there are a lot of things we can all do alone, but that doesn't mean we want to or, for that reason, *have* to."

And so it was settled. He would meet her at Fifty-ninth Street near the Plaza Hotel. They would walk the few blocks to the Women's Center, and he would wait for her until she was stable enough to leave the clinic. They'd take a cab back to her place. Simple.

Except it wasn't. What it was was a feeling of regret and loss. It was Samone's phone ringing at quarter to eight that morning as she checked her wallet for her MasterCard and moved to get her coat. It was Max calling, asking her questions that had arrived too late.

"Why didn't you tell me?" Max began. Samone had told him that she would be busy Saturday and that maybe he could come by Sunday. Had spoken of wanting to go shopping and do some real housecleaning. That he'd just be in the way and hated tagging along behind her as she did A&S and Macy's. That the stores were having a wonderful "after the holiday sale" and she wanted to shop till she dropped.

Not once during this whole barrage had she looked him in the eye, and Max, guilty of much, never pressed her for the truth. Allowed her lies to eat at him most of the night, till morning, when his conscience demanded that he stop her. Demanded that he call her and confront her and tell her, "Don't do it."

"Who told you?"

"I could tell."

"And?"

"Why didn't you just come out and tell me, Samone?"

"Why should I? Is having a baby in your plans?"

"Plans ain't got nothing to do with this."

"Look, I'm going to be late."

"Don't do this, Samone. Don't go. I'm asking you not to."

"Are you marrying me, Max?"

"I don't know." And he really didn't. But that was trivial compared to what she was set to do.

"That's the point. And I'm not ready for single parenting. . . . Look, if I don't leave now, I'm gonna be late. I have to go. Talk to you later."

"Is somebody going with you?"

"Yes."

There were not enough words in the English language to change her mind. Samone was going to get rid of his baby.

"So, I guess I'm not needed."

"No, Max, I guess not. Good-bye."

Max listened to the sound of the call being disconnected. He listened until the buzz went away and a recording told him to hang up, that a phone was off the hook. He listened until a screech replaced the recording. Only then did he hang up the phone.

Max swallowed. Blinked away a sudden wetness in his eye. Because they were tears for the dead, and as of this second, his baby was still alive. Not for long, but alive nonetheless.

He got up and got dressed. He didn't know where

he was going, but he knew he had to get somewhere, soon.

It was supposed to have been so simple. But nothing ever was. First her train was delayed and she had to sit in a tunnel for twenty minutes. During that time the lights went out and the heat died. Samone could only hold herself and try not to think too much.

Jon had not been where he'd said he would be, and she'd nearly missed him when she went to call his house.

The clinic would not honor her credit card because she had left her job ID and other identification at home. Jon ended up using his American Express gold card.

The anesthesia nauseated her, and Samone threw up. It was early afternoon by the time she woke up from the drugged sleep, and she wondered if Jon was still waiting.

He was. With bloodshot eyes and a dazed expression; with Manhattan moving into a sunny afternoon by the time they got onto the street, Jon got them a cab, stopped at the pharmacy, and then took her to his place.

Samone did not want to go to her own.

"Just take it easy, okay? We can talk later," was the last thing Jon said as he pulled the comforter over her.

Some women never asked. Never found the strength to speak the hard question—the question that made the deed real; that gave existence to what no longer existed. But Samone had. Had clutched at the doctor's white coat, licked her dried lips, and asked. The doctor had scanned her chart and told her.

It had been a little girl.

Given the chance, she would have been called Jessica.

Max was cold, and it was getting late. He moved to the phone booth and dialed Pat's number again. Pat picked up on the second ring.

"Any word?"

"No. It's after two. Where in the hell could she be?" On a slim chance, Max had raced over to Samone's gynecologist's office on Madison. But even as he'd waited out front in the cold for her, he'd known that it was the last place she'd go. Eventually he'd gone to her street and set up camp across the way from her building. That had been a while ago.

"I called her mother, and her mother said that she hadn't heard from her, so now I guess I got her momma's worried, too."

"Pat, how could she think she could just up and do this shit without telling me?"

"You? What about me? She ain't never kept no secrets from me . . . I just hope she's okay. I can't think of where in the world she can be."

"Suppose something went wrong? Suppose something's happened to her? Damn it to hell, why didn't I ask, Pat? Why didn't I just ask her?"

"I don't know, Max. I don't know. I'm just trying to figure who went with her," Pat said, stumped.

"She was probably lying. Not wanting me to come."

"How are you doing?"

"Besides scared, hurt, and angry? I'm okay."

"How long you been hanging around there?"

"For a little while."

"How long, Max?"

"I don't know. I got here around eleven."

"And you just been outside all this time?"

"She took back her key."

"Get a cab and come on over."

"Suppose something's wrong?"

"If something's wrong, we'll find out. But right now, you need to get out of the cold."

"On my way."

Samone got out of Jon's bed slowly. It was time to change her pad. She looked at the clock and saw that it was a little after three. The Tylenol with codeine was working; her cramps weren't so bad now.

She went to the bathroom and saw the brown paper bag sitting on the side of the toilet. Inside was a box of Maxithins pads with the flap open. It didn't belong in Jon's bathroom. The more she looked at it, the more it told her so. She pulled down her panties and sat. Heard *ping! ping!* as drops of her blood hit the water. Samone looked at the pad for clots and saw a few. Wondered briefly if it was bits of her baby. Realized it was an awful, terrible thought. Allowed the sadness to wash over her.

I did what I had to do. It couldn't be like that for

me. I won't be a statistic, not even at thirty-five. I won't be a single parent with a boyfriend as the daddy. My momma raised me better. . . . I should call him. Probably worried sick by now. I better call him and let him know that I'm okay.

She moved down the hall toward the living room and found it full of soft light. Afternoon sun glistened off the East River, casting diamonds about the living room. Jon was asleep in the chair, a blanket about his shoulders. His face was turned toward the television, and his lips were parted slightly.

Vulnerable, Samone thought. It wasn't just me on that table today. I took along a whole bunch of people. . . .

She made a move to wake him but decided against it. She went to the phone. It was time to check in. Nobody answered at Max's.

She called Pat.

Max had just hung up from trying Samone's number when the phone rang in his hand. Without thought, he snatched up the receiver.

"Hello?" It was the fear in his voice that halted her tongue. She had not thought Max could be so afraid.

"Hello?" he said again, his pitch high and intense.

Samone wet lips gone dry and readied herself. Swallowed audibly to let him know that someone was on the other end. "I'm okay," she began, her voice betraying its calmness. "I'm at a friend's, but I'm okay."

"Where are you? Why didn't you call sooner? . . . Oh, baby, I was thinking horrible things."

Samone swallowed again, her mouth full of cotton. "I'm at a friend's. I'm fine. I'm just calling to say that, that I'm fine."

"You don't sound 'fine.' Are you sure you're all right? Everything went okay, I mean?"

"It's over."

"But it was okay?"

An abortion is never okay, she wanted to tell him. It's a violation of your body and your soul. Abortion was akin to murder, depending on your viewpoint. No matter how necessary, it would never be "okay."

Samone felt queasy. "I'm fine. I think I better go and lay down now."

"Are you coming home soon?"

"I don't know."

"Who went with you? Where the hell are you?"

"I'm with a friend. Tell Pat, okay? Tell her I'm fine."

Samone hung up.

"Hi." Jon's voice came as it should have, soft and fragile. He knew that words could hurt her. She looked up and saw him standing at the kitchen entrance and wondered how long he had been watching her.

"Hello," she managed, before she pulled her eyes away.

"Feeling better?"

She nodded, unable to speak any more lies.

"I think I'm going to go out and get some Chinese.

You want something? Some soup, maybe?''

Samone nodded again. It was too hard to speak now.

''Why don't you get back in bed till I get back.''

''Yeah, okay.''

Jon got his jacket, glad to get out of the apartment.

It was a glorious Saturday, where the sun was high, the temperatures moderate, and sunlight dappled against everything. It was the kind of day where Jon loved to go to the Village and window-shop. Eat pizza on Eighth Street and browse through books on astrology.

It was the type of day where he would take in a movie or do his laundry. Not spend all morning in an abortion clinic; misplaced anger sizzling around and about him simply because he was a man. Jon being the other half of the equation of why women ended up in places like that.

Which led him to analyze how ''responsible'' he had been. That night he had slept with Samone, he had used a condom against sexual diseases, not out of any great need to prevent what had happened to her anyway. He didn't understand how a woman as smart and intelligent as she could wind up in this situation. And where the hell was Max?

What kind of bogeyman had Samone fallen in love with? What kind of man did Samone love that she couldn't even tell she was carrying his child? That she was doing this in secret? This most sacred part of loving?

Jon had been holding it back most of the morning,

but now that the morning was over, he could not stop his bitterness. Yesterday, when he had volunteered, he had been feeling very white knight–ish and "that's what friends are for." He had not expected Samone to end up at his house.

He had not expected to care beyond her immediate well-being. He had not expected his anger or his condemnation. If she had been with him, it would have never happened.

It was this last thought that had him. That for all the tea in China, it would still be Max that Samone would love.

He found her looking out the living room window, the Queens shoreline looming in the distance.

"What are you doing up?"

"Couldn't lie down anymore."

"I thought you said you had to lie down for a while."

"I did and now I'm up."

"You just had surgery, for God's sake." It was not the words that wounded. It was his tone full of all those things that she did not expect and could not use. Full of hostility and insinuation. Full of blame.

A tear rolled down her face. She allowed herself that. She watched him until he was forced to look away. Only then did she speak.

"People make mistakes, Jon. I made a mistake. Poor judgment. Whatever you want to call it. Do I need to be persecuted? Haven't I been through enough? . . . I thought you were my friend. Asked you if you were and you told me 'yes.' Told me, 'Yes,

Samone, you're the only real friend I have in New York.' So be it. Just be a friend. Not a judge or a fucking jury. A friend.''

Even you, Jon? Last person I'd expect something from is you. How *dare* he. She walked past him.

''Where are you going?''

She headed toward the closet. Her coat was inside.

''Home.''

''You haven't even eaten. At least eat first.''

''No.'' Samone grabbed the doorknob and gave it a twist. So what if it wasn't her closet. Her coat was inside, and she'd be damned if she'd ask permission to get it.

''Samone. Come on. You just can't walk out of here with nothing in your stomach.'' She couldn't leave angry at *him*. It was Max she needed to be flying off the handle at.

''Samone, you can't leave.''

''Who says I can't?'' The closet door was now open. Clothes unfamiliar and tightly packed greeted her. Could she really find her coat in there? She hesitated, her hand in midair, unsure where to begin.

''Wait, just wait, please.''

She did. Not because she wanted to, but the moment did not allow her to continue. She turned and looked at him. He returned her look. Did not back down from her intense gaze. Softened his demeanor two notches, weighing his words carefully.

''Hate my guts, call me names. But please, don't leave here without something to eat . . . please?''

And there it was. The reason she had sought him.

The compassion and concern that was deep and warranted. The one thing she could never use, until now. There, right there in his eyes, in the sadness of his face. *Right there, Samone.*

She turned away from the thought. "Okay," she said without surrender.

Samone stepped back and away from the closet, closed the door. Moved to the kitchen to eat the soup and go. Forgiving but not forgetting, not ever, she decided. *Because even now, Jon, as you carefully find me a spoon and take out the container of soup, you still are holding me accountable. I'm still guilty in your book. Even as you play nice-nice with me, you still feel it's my fault. And that I will never forgive, not ever.*

Taking the spoon offered, Samone lifted the lid off the container of egg-drop soup. As she shook in the fried noodles, some spilled onto the white Formica counter. Her fingers collected them quickly and brought them to her mouth.

The soup burned her tongue, but she didn't care. Samone took in spoonful after spoonful. She was hungry, but most important, she had to get out of there.

Jon watched her eat, feeling her anxiety and her need to get away from him.

Jon got her things as she finished the last of the soup. Had her coat and her bag ready as she turned from dumping the container into the garbage. Helped her into her leather. Stepped back to allow her access to the door. Spoke as her hand reached the knob, his voice full and intent against her back. She never turned to face him.

"This is the last thing I wanted for you. So if I come off a little pissed, well, God forgive me, I'm human. But I'm hurting as much as you, and I really don't want you to leave like this." He paused. "I just wanted you to know that."

Samone flurried her fingers in the air. She had no use for his words, so she rebuked them. Left them behind. Because what he felt was the least of her concerns.

It had gotten cold. The air was brittle and freezing. Samone had tried to hail three cabs; none of them had stopped.

She grasped the collar of her coat and walked to the next block. Felt something warm gush between her legs. The cold weather wasn't doing anything for her cramps, either.

She stood there, frantically waving her hand at the endless parade of metered cabs. Five more cabs passed by before one stopped. The driver was a Brother and had no problems taking her where she wanted to go. Harlem didn't scare him.

She dozed. And in what seemed like minutes, the cabbie was waking her up. On the sidewalk, she gazed up the street. She needed sanitary napkins, something she had not used since high school. Unlike most of her friends, Samone hadn't been afraid to try tampons. She had dismissed the myth that said if you used a tampon, "you wouldn't be a virgin no more."

Since tenth grade she had used them, so there wasn't a single sanitary pad in her house. Remembered the box left beside Jon's toilet and wondered what he would do with them. The bodega on the corner stocked them. She headed up the street.

Samone was weak by the time she got back to her building. Juggling her pocketbook and package, she began to search for the first of two keys needed to let herself in. She was about to slip the first into the lock when she heard a voice.

"I'm sorry that I have not shared enough of myself with you to trust me with this . . . that's all I wanted to say."

"Max?" Samone turned, keys and bag falling from her fingers. "Oh, Max."

Tears had been constant for Max most of the day. Mostly when the pain came and he forgot that men didn't cry. When he remembered that their baby was dead and so was their love.

But Samone had never seen him cry. She leaned into him. "Don't cry, Max. Please don't cry."

"I feel soo bad, Samone. I feel so bad."

"I know. Come on. Let's go in."

The apartment, dark, silent, and warm, was like arms about them both.

"Did you eat today?" he asked, dabbing his eye with the side of his palm.

Samone thought about the soup and recalled Jon's anger. Told herself that that had been a hundred years ago, no longer in her lifetime.

"Some soup, not much else."

"Why don't you lay down and I'll make you something."

"I don't want to lay down. Been laying down all day. What I want is a hot shower, my flannels, and to curl up on my couch and get on with my life. I'm tired of being a victim."

"Go ahead. I'll be here . . . we have to talk."

Samone nodded and headed toward the back.

We have to talk.

The hot water felt good on her body. She stood there a long time, tips of her hair getting wet, water beating on her face.

Samone turned, the water moving over her shoulders. She closed her eyes and leaned against the cool ceramic tiles.

We have to talk.

She reached for the bar of soap and lathered up her palms. Moved the bubbles over her arms, under her breasts. Lathered her palms again and washed her stomach, her thighs. Between her legs.

Talk.

The bathroom was steamy, misty, and warm. Surrounding her, protecting her. Comforting her.

Talk.

Samone turned off the shower and reached for a towel. Wrapped herself up and stepped out of the tub. Cleared the bathroom mirror, looking at her reflection.

She toweled herself off, slipping into clean panties, a fresh pad, and her flannel pajamas. Slipped on her white terry-cloth robe and into her bedroom slippers. Reached for the doorknob.

Fear had driven her to this minute, this second, in her life. Fear of rejection, fear of not being loved enough, and fear of not being able to be forgiven.

Samone twisted the knob and pulled open the door, steam rushing past her into the hall.

You couldn't love in fear. Couldn't love somebody being afraid. It made you do unwise things, foolish things . . . getting pregnant . . . foolish things . . . sneaking off to get an abortion.

She heard Max in the kitchen. Was sitting on the couch when he appeared with a cup of tea. "Put some lemon in it," he said, handing it to her.

She took the cup, curled her feet up under her, and readied herself for Max to begin. She knew what he had to say and was no longer afraid.

"Feeling better?" he asked.

Samone nodded, eyes away from him, wishing he would take a seat, knowing that he wouldn't.

Max sighed, massaging his eyes. "What a day"— he looked at her—"just madness, pure and simple." He shook his head. "I must of waited outside your apartment for two hours"—he smiled somberly— "freezing my cans off. Not knowing where the hell you were."

Samone would not apologize.

He talked on. "I've never been so scared in my life. Not knowing where you were, but what you were doing."

Samone sipped her tea.

"Wishing," he continued, "wishing I could take it all back and do it over." He looked at her again. "But I couldn't, and of course, there was no stopping you. Made no sense to me at first. Getting pregnant, and then trying to sneak an abortion." He laughed in self-pity. "Had to think about what that said about me . . . not a hell of a lot. You know I knew, suspected, same difference, should have opened up my mouth then. Couldn't."

The tea was hot. Samone put it down.

"I didn't want you to get pregnant, but no way in hell did I want you to have an abortion."

"I didn't know that, Max," Samone said, speaking for the first time. "All I knew was you didn't want to get married and I couldn't be a single parent."

"But you never even asked me, Samone."

"You never asked *me*."

"That's not even the point."

"It's exactly the point, okay? Christmas morning, that's when I decided. Hell of a day to choose, isn't it. I opened that box and saw a bracelet. Knew you still didn't want to marry me and a baby would have made it worse."

It was the first time he raised his voice.

"Knew? *Knew?* Samone, you knew shit . . . you knew what you wanted to know and that was it. You knew shit, you hear me?" How could she not hear him? His voice was loud and thunderous. But Samone was determined not to be sucked in. She settled the fear inside of her.

"Shit," he continued. "Mutherfuck," he said to no

one, his voice winding down as tears swelled in his eyes. He tapped his chest. "How could you do this to me? All this time we were together, didn't you know me better? I would have done whatever it took. Would have done whatever the fuck it took to make it work. No damn abortion, not ever." He put his face in his hands and sobbed.

Samone blinked away the wetness in her eyes, her jaw moving, determined not to join him in his pity. She had been the one lying up on the table today, not him. He'd had his chance and he'd blown it. End of fucking story.

Her voice trembled. "All you had to do was ask me. You knew I was scared to death and wouldn't tell unless you asked. But no, you played the waiting game. You could have called me Friday night, but no, you chose Saturday morning, knowing damn well where I was going and what I was going to do. So don't be expecting no fucking sympathy from me, okay? I was the one on that table today, not you. I'm the one who has to live with this the rest of my life, not you . . . killed my baby because I didn't want to lose you, do you understand? Because I didn't want to lose you. What a fucking joke."

Max blinked, Samone's words sobering him. He knew she was absolutely right. He looked around him as if looking for something he had lost. Wiped his eyes, coughed. Sniffled.

"Well," he said in his best director of mortgage voice, "guess there's no more to say. Better be on my way."

"Yeah, guess you should," Samone said, hating him. Seeing all of his weakness and all of her strengths.

He looked at her, pained. "Didn't know each other as well as we thought, did we."

"Guess not."

"You take care of yourself, okay?"

"Yes, I will," Samone said, determined.

He turned, getting his coat, slipping it on. Fighting the need to cry, Samone was determined to let Max walk. No scenes, no drama, just let him go.

Out of her life, forever and for the last time.

"Good-bye," he said, meaning it.

"Bye," Samone responded, knowing she had no choice but to agree.

10

The garbage was full to the brim. Not another thing could fit in the plastic bag. And there was grease around her stove burners from the bacon Samone had fried that morning. She looked at the wall clock, knowing that any moment Pat would be buzzing the intercom. Even between best friends, a clean apartment was everything. But there just wasn't enough time.

She got her keys and slipped on the bedroom slippers that had seen better days. As she walked up the hall to the incinerator, she could hear *Soul Train* played loudly on her neighbor Lanie's TV, and the smell of curry and spices meant Frieda was making her Saturday cook-up. The incinerator was jammed with garbage, and normally Samone would take time to force her garbage down, but this wasn't a "normal" time for her.

There were other things more important for her consideration, for her concern. So she left the bag on the floor and closed the steel door.

As she passed the elevator the doors opened and Samone looked instinctively over her shoulder. Pat stepped out, concern and worry deep across the bridge of her forehead, in the slim ridge of flesh where the wool hat ended and her eyebrows began.

Samone smiled. She hated that hat.

"I came in behind somebody else."

"I was just emptying the garbage. Come on. You hungry? I bought some cold cuts."

"I ate. Ray was in a good mood. Made breakfast and did the dishes afterward."

"What? Not your husband."

"Yeah, honey. The very same one."

The apartment was full of winter light. A soft focused haze eased around corners and settled on the pale walls. Lysol permeated the air, and Pat knew Samone had been cleaning. It was something Pat would have been doing, but today her alliances were elsewhere.

"Me and Max have said good-bye," Samone told her, striking a match, the sulfur rushing across the sandpaper causing sparks and a flame of white and blue.

"Yeah . . . I know."

"That was a few days ago." She laughed bitterly, self-consciously. "Of course I woke up in the morning wanting to change my mind, even though I knew better.''

"Love ain't never easy, Sam."

"Love? This ain't about love. It's about what Max wants and when he wants it. All he can see is I didn't tell him. Pat, don't you think I wanted to tell him? I was afraid . . . I didn't do it because I hated him. I did it because I didn't want to lose him."

"Well," Pat conceded, easing back against the sofa, nudging the leather sneakers off her feet, "it's all over now."

"Sometimes I'm not so sure." And Samone wasn't. She couldn't say that if Max walked in the door that second, she wouldn't want to take him back.

She changed the subject. "I see you got your hair done." Black people had hair fetishes. Most women wanted it long and real. And those who couldn't grow it usually bought it. There was money to be made in black hair.

Pat had put braid extensions in her hair. They fell about her face and shoulder soft and easy. Unconsciously she fingered a few.

"You know how winter does my hair, the little I don't have. Stuff comes out in handfuls. Figure I'd keep them in till spring. 'Course, you never had that problem."

In fairness, Samone hadn't. It had fallen beyond her shoulders since she could remember, and not even a salon's shears could keep it short for any long period of time. It was an envy of Pat's.

"Where'd you go?"

"Senegalese sisters down on a Hundred Twenty-fifth Street. Those women get down with some braiding. Their fingers be flying, and before you know it, they're through."

"Yeah, it's definitely time for a touch-up. My briar patch is so nappy, honey, I can hardly get a comb through it. Of course, now it'll have to wait. I'm broke."

"The abortion?" It was the first time Pat had spoken the word to Samone. It colored the room in hues of mauve, full of sadness and regret.

"Yeah. I didn't want the job to know my business, so I was gonna pay for it, but then I forgot my ID, and they wouldn't take my MasterCard. Thank God for Jon."

It was out of her mouth before she could check it. Pat's eyes grew dark, full of resentment.

"Jon? What's he got to do with this?"

"Forget it, Pat. Just forget it."

"I asked you a question, Samone."

"And I ain't answering it. So just drop it."

"He's the one. The one who went with you. . . . Now ain't this some shit. Here I am, been your damn best friend since forever, and you go and trust some fucking white boy. Over me, Samone? Over Max?"

"Pat, it's not like that."

"Bullshit, Samone. Fucking bullshit."

Samone stood up, angry and wearied. She was tired of apologizing for every move she made. The air was thick with electricity as Pat stared, waiting. It could have been long time ago, when Pat had cornered her in the high school locker room. Samone felt the hairs on her neck rise.

She knew Pat's bitterness was fever pitch. But Samone was ready to do battle.

"Look, it ain't like you think. He's a friend. Nothing more. And no, I didn't want anybody to know. You think if I had, I wouldn't have told you from jump street? You would have been the first, even before Max. But I didn't want nobody to know"—Samone's voice was butter—"...can you understand that? I didn't want people blaming me. I just wanted to go and get it over. And I knew I couldn't do it alone. So, yeah. I told Jon. I told a fucking white boy over you. Not because I wanted to...I *had* to...."

Samone paused, taking a cleansing breath. "You would have told Max, I know you would have. You would not have been able not to tell him. It's your way, Pat...so I had to look for an alternative...I didn't do it for spite or to hurt nobody. I did it because I felt it was best."

Pat sniffled, a quick hand against the corner of her eye. Licked her lips, looked away. Swallowed.

"I'm sorry. Guess I've been as much of an ass as Max. I'm really sorry."

Without thought, Pat was standing. In her mind she was already reaching out to Samone, taking her into her arms whether Samone wanted it or not. In her mind they were already hugging and forgiving each other. Letting their arms speak of unconditional absolution with no strings attached.

It felt good to be hugged. Seemingly not in a hundred years had anybody hugged Samone for no other reason than that was what her body required. Samone longed to stay there in her friend's arms. Longed to stay even though her mind was telling her she was too old to be this needy. To old to be rocked and cuddled. Slow to let go, they pulled apart.

Pat, laughing quick and caught, looked around her for distraction. Samone reached for her smoldering cigarette, in need to be doing something other.

Then Samone was speaking of hunger and hero bread with lots of mustard, mayo, and deli meat. Pat started talking about honey ham and Swiss and how she hoped that was what Samone had bought, 'cause "you know that's my favorite."

"Of course. What else did you ever eat besides honey ham and Swiss?"

Jon sat in the control room, Abe, his technical director, on his left side, Jane, the executive director, on his right. They had been looking over new show logos for the past half hour.

Jon stared at the monitor. "Abe, pull up the last one." He watched the image appear, nodded his head.

Getting there.

"What do you think, Jane?"

She played with her pearls, twisted her mouth, and screwed up her eyes. "Almost . . . still needs something. Maybe making the logo bigger, different colors . . . something."

"Abe, pull up the color schemes." The monitor showed the *New York Live* logo in various colors.

"I like the red one," Abe offered, though he wasn't asked.

Jane shook her head. "No, too racy. Now that peach one is a nice color."

"For TV?" Jon shook his head. "No. I think we should stick with the—"

The control room speakers sizzled. "Jon, call on line seven."

"Excuse me," Jon said, picking up the phone. "Jonathon Everette speaking."

"Busy?"

His heart fell to the floor. The last person he expected to hear from; the only one he wanted to hear from.

"Wondering if we could meet for lunch," Samone asked.

Jon looked around, saw his co-workers listening without appearing to be.

"Can't today. Dinner?"

"Can't. Tomorrow?"

Jon looked at his watch. "You have appointments this afternoon?"

"Free from three on."

"Three? Your office?"

"Sure."

Jon got off the elevator, moved swiftly down the quiet hall, and pushed open the glass doors. He caught Merissa's eyes and gave a wink. Merissa winked back. She liked Jon.

He continued around the corner and knocked on Samone's office door.

"Enter."

"Hey," Jon offered.

"Hey back," Samone said, her face creased. "I'm sorry, Jon, for going off on you. Wasn't you I should have been mad at."

He nodded, glad she understood. "I know."

Samone shook her head. "What a nightmare, huh? Thank God it's over."

He spied her with a questioning look. "Is it?"

"What?"

"Over?"

Samone looked away, sighed. "Yep. Finished and done."

He took a seat. "So, how are you doing?"

Samone shrugged. "Could be better, could be worse."

"Well, you're looking great, as always."

Samone smiled whimsically. "Yeah, so you say."

He studied her a minute. "Everything else is fine, though? I mean, you're okay?"

"As okay as it gets, I guess. . . ." Her eyes went to his, her head shaking in disbelief. "You were so good Saturday."

"Long as you're okay. All that matters." And those eyes, those tiger eyes, were full upon her.

11

Valentine's Day arrived on a cold Tuesday morning. Samone was trying hard to forget this day of love, but the single red rose on her desk made that impossible. There wasn't a card, and she assumed it was from the CEO doing his thing—turkeys for Thanksgiving, bottles of inexpensive champagne for New Year's Eve. Four-leaf clovers for St. Patrick's Day.

Roses for Valentine's Day?

She asked Merissa about it when she ran into her in the ladies' room.

"Was there a rose on your desk this morning?"

Merissa's right eyebrow rose up defiantly. "What rose?"

"You didn't get one?"

Merissa kept combing her hair, as though it were all she ever did. The eyebrow dropped swiftly back into place right before she gave her answer.

"No, I didn't."

Later, Samone asked her co-worker Claire the same question.

"No. I didn't get a rose, why?"

Just me? Samone shook her head. "No reason," she mumbled, heading for her office.

Later . . .

"Samone Lewis?"

It had been a busy morning. Everybody was in need of work. Samone was taking a quick cigarette break when she looked up and saw the badly dressed man in the shiny black pants and runned-over shoes standing in her doorway, a white box, half his height, pressed against his belly.

"Yes."

"I have a delivery. Can you sign, please?"

"Who are they from?"

"Have to read the card, ma'am." He placed the receipt on her desk. Pointed toward the bottom of the invoice. "Sign here."

She scribbled her name and realized two things at once: there were at least half a dozen roses inside, and she was important on somebody's Valentine's Day.

Samone opened the box. A dozen yellow roses.

Only two people in the whole world knew that she preferred yellow over red: her mother and Max.

Then the other rose had to be from Jon.

Even as she gathered them up, inhaling their fragrant bouquet, even as she found a vase, blew dust from its bottom, and went to fill it with water, the other had her attention.

One single red rose, holding her captive.

After arranging the yellow ones the best she could, Samone picked up the phone, dialed the number, and bit her longest nail to the quick. "Angela? It's Samone. Max there?"

"Hold on, Samone. He's in a meeting, but he told me to disturb him if you called. Hold on."

Less than twenty seconds Max was on the phone. "You got them?"

"What?" Teasing him because she could.

"Is this Samone Lewis?"

"Yes."

"Oh. I thought so. Did you like them?"

"Very much."

"My apology . . . for everything," he told her.

"Don't matter now. Ancient history, right?" Samone asked, holding on deep to that truth.

There was a pause, and she knew Max was no surer than she was. "You're about right. . . . Look, we said some things—"

Samone cut him off. "Uh-uh, don't do that. Forward, let's not go back."

"Okay." More pausing. "I, I got to get back—"

"To your meeting, yes, I know. Thanks for the roses."

"You're more than welcome," he told her.

*   *   *

Only her conceit had her last minute waiting for Jon in the office lobby. Only her conceit had her assuming that just because she hadn't wanted to be with him, somebody else wouldn't.

Jon was handsome, middle class, and male. *What makes you think he's gonna be by himself just 'cause he ain't with you?*

She didn't. All she knew was her feet started moving the moment she spotted him. Regardless of what he was or wasn't doing, she was going to walk up to him. Smile, speak, and give him the rose.

"Special delivery for Jonathon Everette."

Jon took the rose, brought it to his nose, his eyes fast on her, surprised and joyful. "My first."

"You're kidding."

Jon shook his head. "Nope. First and only. Thanks."

"Welcome."

"Where you headed?" he asked.

"Nowhere. Home."

"But it's Valentine's Day."

Samone nodded. "I know."

"Dinner?" he asked.

"Sure. I'd love to."

It was so warm in the restaurant, Samone wanted to close her eyes and just lean against the wall. Instead she watched Jon approach her, his shaking head telling her bad news.

"No sitting, no standing. No nothing."

"But this is the fourth place we tried. Don't they

have takeout?'' Samone wanted to know.

"I don't think so.''

Samone looked around. The smell of food everywhere but on an available plate.

"Now what?''

"I know this deli. Nothing fancy, but they have homemade soup and wonderful sandwiches.''

"No sandwiches, Jon. I want a meal.''

"I have steaks in the freezer. I can toss a salad, nuke some potatoes. Pick up some Italian bread and a bottle of wine?''

"Sounds real good.'' Besides, it was the only place they really needed to be.

With the last bit of Italian bread, Samone sopped up the steak sauce and popped it into her mouth. Wiped her lips and leaned back.

"Forget the cheesecake.'' She patted her full stomach. "There's no more room in this inn.''

"Nothing else I can get you?''

Samone stood up from the table, gathering her drink. "A cab and a bed, in that order.''

"You ready to go?''

No, she liked where she was. Jon was so easy to get with. It was so easy being in his space.

Samone shook her head. Pursed her lips. "No, not yet.''

"What? TV? Music?''

"Yeah, put on the Lee Ritenour CD again. I like that one.''

"Ah, yes. 'Dolphin Dream' and 'Malibu.' ''

"Malibu" had been Jon and Yvonne's song. Tonight was the first time that he'd played it in a while.

"Yeah," she said, her head lifted, her mouth not quite closed, tasting the melody, "that's the one."

Curled up on his couch with her bare feet tucked beneath her, there wasn't nothing wrong with her world. It had been a long time since she felt so free . . . she savored it. Took sips of Jon's silence and the fullness of his presence; of the song moving around her, full of love.

Samone indulged herself, quiet and reclusive in the simple luxury of "nothing matters but now." Her eyes grew soft and tender.

From the other end of the sofa, Jon smiled at her. His eyes shimmered like a hundred jewels.

"What's so funny?" Samone asked, still caught in her gentle solitude.

"Nothing. Just watching you."

Samone shifted; the spell, wavering. "What do you see?"

"The different yous."

Samone laughed, the sound like the tinkle of a crystal.

"Is that good or bad?"

"Tonight, it's very good."

Jon reached out, caressed her hair. Her head leaned into the gentle motion. She closed her eyes and sighed. Said two words full of bittersweet longing, her eyes speaking what she could not.

"Oh, Jon."

"I know.

But he didn't, not really. The idea made her laugh and sit up. She studied him before releasing what had been on her tongue since forever.

"Ever wanted to be black, Jon?"

He didn't pause to answer. "No."

Her smile shifted, lopsided and full of mischief. "Just want to bop black women."

Yes, she was pushing him, and over the edge they'd go tonight. A part of her was curious how far she'd take it; a part of her already knew.

"Is that what you think?" Jon asked.

It didn't matter what she *thought*. What mattered was why she was here and what he felt he needed that only she could give.

"It's true, isn't it."

"Are you asking me or telling me, Samone?"

Her eyes lit upon him, daring him to tell a lie. "I'm asking."

"What, if I want to sleep with you?"

When she understood that Jon was willing to take the conversation as far as she was, she quit the game. Switched moods. Pulled back.

"You did, remember?" Her coup de grâce.

"Touché."

And then the words of the song moved about them, full of longing and that special place where two hearts met. The melody, the sorrow-timbred voice, surrounded them both, and in need of asylum, Samone started talking. "Didn't you live in Malibu?"

Her fear was showing, and Jon took advantage. He asked her to dance.

"Dance? What, are you crazy?" There was panic in her voice.

"Listen to those lyrics, Samone. How can you resist?" He coaxed her to her feet, ignoring her protests.

"Come on, it's Valentine's Day. . . ." His voice, honey sweet.

Slow dancing? How long had it been? Had she ever danced slow with a man in his apartment instead of some crowded dance floor? It was something most men would not ask. But Jon was not most men.

So she went, her pensive smile telling of how close he could get and where he could place his hands. Up close, her chin came to his collarbone. Up close, his cologne was full of sweet promise. Up close, she felt his nature rise.

They danced close. Tight. He kissed her. A tear gathered on the edges of her eyelids, slipped past her lashes.

"Don't cry," was all he said, as if he understood. But Samone knew he didn't understand a damn thing, and she moved out of his arms. It was time for her to go.

"I'm ready for that cab."

So Jon called a car service and started the dishes. Samone kept him company as he scrubbed the broiling pan and wiped off the kitchen counter.

As Jon went about his kitchen chores, he realized that Samone was carefully watching the next man she would love.

He wondered if she knew.

12

Samone had seen him watching her from six yards away. Knew the smile he gave as they passed had been ready from the moment he spotted her. She understood her lure and her power today. He wasn't the first stranger who smiled at her as she made her way down Fifth Avenue.

"Now, he was fine," Samone decided, her head following his passing.

"Should have said hi."

"I just want to look, not take 'em home, Pat."

"I told you to wear your coat. You're damn near about to stop traffic."

"Well, let me stop it, then. I feel good today. The sun is out and it's hot and I'm about ready to run across Fifth Avenue butt naked. God, I love this time of the year."

"Is it the 'time of year' or that you can walk around showing everybody your stuff?"

"Both, probably. I mean, spring is here, child, and I'm ready."

Pat gave her a strange look. "For . . . ?"

"Whatever. Whatever life is offering me."

"Well, that didn't take long."

"What, Pat?"

"You know, you realizing that the world still spins without Max."

"I always knew that. But on a day like today, I can believe it."

Samone was feeling good. About damn time, was all she knew.

"Anything new?" Pat asked, not expecting it to be. Because Samone would have been on the phone with her about it for sure.

"No. Nothing much. Going to the movies this weekend."

"Oh, yeah? With who?"

"Jon."

"Oh, the white boy."

"Yeah, the white boy. He's not bad, Pat. He's a cool white guy."

"And after the movies?"

"My business."

"Ah, shit. You gonna give him some."

"Now how do you know that?"

" 'Cause I know you. Been a long time, and you were never one to say no when your body means yes."

"Fuck you, Patricia."

"You wish you could." For a second or two they glared at each other. Then Pat smiled, and Samone returned the favor, snatching up Pat's arm.

"Come on. We're gonna miss the light." They were in the middle of the street when the light changed. Samone never looked back. Not even as drivers slammed on their brakes and cursed them out loud.

She knew nobody was going to hit her. Not with the kind of legs she was sporting.

When you've been with a man a while, you knew what to wear to whatever function came up. Samone hadn't been anywhere with Jon except after work, so she didn't have a clue. And Jon wasn't telling.

"Come on, Jon. Give me a hint. I mean, I'm over here looking at a whole bunch of stuff, and I don't have the slightest idea about what you're gonna be wearing."

"Look, you've been to the movies before on a Saturday night. Just act like it's business as usual."

"I've been to the movies, yes, but somehow what you wear and what my other dates wore don't seem like quite the same thing."

"Wear whatever you want."

"Are you sure this is a good movie?"

"Absolutely."

"Apartment fourteen D, and don't be late."

"I know. I wrote it down. See you at nine sharp."

Movies with Jon on a Saturday night. A real date.

She had yet to tell her momma about him. Could not imagine what her daddy would say.

Time to get busy.

She still had to set her hair and do her nails. Press her black demins and shower steam her cable-knit sweater. Do her makeup and decide if she was going to wear perfume or not.

Jon was prompt. She liked that.

Samone also liked his 501 jeans and sable leather jacket. Even his hair was combed differently, making him look less serious and younger.

So far, so good, Samone thought.

They took a cab at her insistence and rode downtown as New York City glittered and gleamed by at a dizzying pace.

"You look nice."

Samone mumbled, "thank you," looking away.

Jon took her chin. "No. I mean it. You look wonderful."

"Yeah. Sure. All I want to know is, who's paying?"

He laughed, releasing her, the need to kiss her no less real.

"You're good, Samone. Real good."

Smiling, her face a quick flash of warmth in the flickering darkness, Samone agreed, "I know."

He bought her popcorn, a drink, and chocolate bonbons and didn't complain when she ate half of his Raisinets. He didn't try to hold her hand, and he wasn't a talker. Samone liked that. She was feeling pretty good as they stood outside the movie theater afterward.

Jon looked up the avenue. "You want to go somewhere else? Like for a drink or something?"

"No. I have to take a rain check."

"But it's still early."

"Quarter to twelve isn't early, Jon."

"It's not that late. I know this great bar on Second Avenue, what do you say?"

"It's kinda late. And I have to go all the way up-town."

"You can always get a cab."

"After a certain time, cabs don't go to Harlem."

"I'll flag it, take the ride up with you, if you want."

"You don't have to ride up with me, but I'm gonna have to give you a rain check on drinks." *Movies is fine and all, but I've been to those bars you want to take me to. Nothing but a bunch of loud-ass white people, listening to loud-ass white music, talking about their loud-ass white lives.*

Yeah, I can just see me stroll in there with you. No, they wouldn't stare long. But every time an ofay laughed out loud, I'd think they were laughing at us. . . . Thanks, but no thanks. Besides, I might end up in the wrong place, like your place. . . . It was such a nice evening. Don't rush me. Don't rush me and spoil it. And don't get that look on your face. I'm here, aren't I?

"The bar's not far," Jon offered.

"Jon, look. Before we have another fight, which

would be a real shame, because I had such a nice time, let me set the record straight. You asked me to the movies and I was happy to go. That was our date. Drinks and all that stuff, I'm just not up to. All right?''

Jon smiled tightly, his eyes hard and shielded. ''Sure, let's get you a cab.''

He moved into the street, raised his right hand, and yelled, ''Taxi!'' One stopped right away. He opened the door, and the cabbie did not realize Samone was in the backseat by herself until he turned to ask, ''Where to?''

She almost said, ''Harlem,'' but, thinking better, she gave her address.

The taxi driver gave them both a dirty look. Jon stared back, asking, ''Is that a problem?''

The cabbie turned on his meter, not answering.

''See you Monday.'' Jon closed the door.

Yeah, Samone thought, *see you Monday. But then what?*

13

The delicate sounds of violins came up from the cobbled path. Sunlight dappled, birds chirped. Cherry blossoms let loose their fragrant bounty, and the smell of fresh-turned earth heralded the arrival of spring.

Central Park was in all its glory, and Samone, in no rush to leave, closed her eyes and sighed. Lunch, a quick meal of hot dogs and C&C grape soda, had been eaten on the way. To get out into the beautiful day was the real reason behind this hour away from work.

"I could stay here forever. Isn't it a glorious day?" she asked Jon. But he merely nodded, the play of sunshine through the leaves more important than his need to speak.

It *had* been different since that night at the movies. They still did lunch, but Jon had pulled back, which suited Samone just fine. No sex, no pressure. Just friends.

Samone felt safe again. Didn't have to worry about hurting his feelings or telling him no.

Today his mood was more somber than usual. Not even the good weather moved him. Samone spoke what had been obvious from the moment they'd met in the lobby for lunch.

"You're awfully quiet," Samone said.

"Am I?"

"No, Jon, I'm lying. What's up? You haven't talked about one person and cracked a stupid-ass joke since we got here."

"I met somebody."

Samone blinked, a jackhammer slamming into her chest. She struggled to keep her face straight as her mind got busy with the news Jon just told. *I met somebody.*

So that was it. Jon found the somebody that Samone wouldn't be. And in her conceit of who she was to him, she hadn't even noticed.

"Oh, yeah? Who?" she managed, hiding nothing behind her raised eyebrow, as though she were really glad about this news Jon had kept to himself.

He wouldn't look at her. "Her name's Daryn."

"A girl name Darren?"

"Well, you spell it different."

"So when did this happen?"

"The night we went to the movies."

"I see."

"It's not how it sounds." But it was exactly how

it sounded. Samone wouldn't sleep with him, so Jon went and found someone who would.

There had been other women, Samone was almost certain. But Jon never mentioned them, and Samone figured they weren't important.

This Darren must have been special. She was the only one Jon had ever told her about.

Samone shrugged, looked around. Forced herself not to care. Knew that sooner or later it would come to this.

Everybody needed to be loved. Jon was no different. *Samone* was no different. She didn't want Jon's love, but a part of her needed it. It gave her a sense of self; that who and what she was was important.

But it was changing right before her eyes. Jon had found someone else, and soon she wouldn't matter to him at all.

Samone stood. "We better head back, it's getting late." Looked up the cobbled path. How many more lunches before we don't do this at all? she wondered, missing him already.

Missing him in a way she never thought she could.

Samone's mother fingered the rayon blouse, eyed the tag, and clucked her teeth. She put the shirt back on the rack.

"You need a ride? Uncle Chicken said he would pick you up if you did."

"Probably. Don't see how else I'm gonna get there." Time was moving on, quicksilver and without her. Already it was Friday before Memorial Day. Already.

Since January, in need of winter relief, Samone had begun to look forward to her family's Memorial Day picnic. Had looked forward to being among longtime-no-see cousins and aunts who looked like her.

She had purchased a black latex bikini, not knowing if it would be hot enough to get in the pool but knowing she'd look damn good in it. So far so good. Summer was coming in early. Still, there were things that not even a serious shiny skintight bikini could fix. She was thirty-five and dateless.

"Hear from Max?" her mother asked, sixth sense.

"No, Mom. I told you, it's really over between us."

"Holidays do funny things, Samone. Maybe you should call him."

"So I won't be alone Monday? Mom. Please."

"Okay, I'll shut up. God, look at the time. I know your father's wondering where in the world I am."

"Shopping with his daughter at Macy's on a Friday afternoon. Where else?"

"Come on, I want to check upstairs. I saw a nice easy chair I think your father might tolerate."

"Now, Mom, you know he loves the one he's had since I was in eighth grade."

"Yeah, and every time he sits in it, I keep hoping it'll just fall completely apart."

"Let's take the elevator. The escalator takes forever."

*   *   *

"Mom, Daddy's gonna have your head."

"I just want to check one more thing. Your father really can use another pair of white slacks."

"Oh, no. Not the white slacks."

"It's tradition. White slacks for all the summer holidays."

"I'm just glad they're back in fashion."

They were approaching the cologne counter. Without thinking, Samone stopped and searched until she found the tester bottle of Polo. Was bringing it up to her nose when her eyes caught Jon across the counter.

The bottle slipped from her grip and clattered to the glass top. Embarrassed and trapped, Samone forced her mouth shut and then open as she fumbled for words to speak.

"Jon? What are you doing here? I mean, I know what you're doing here, but what are you doing here?" She became aware of her mother beside her. But before she could consider how to introduce them, her mother did what she sensed Samone wouldn't.

"Hello, I'm Jessica Lewis."

But Jon knew that. The striking older black woman could be no one else. She and Samone were cut from the same cloth.

Samone, flustered, gathered her thoughts and made apologies. "My manners. Mom, this is Jon, he works at NBS."

"Nice to meet you, Mrs. Lewis." Jon smiled, and Jessica nodded, watching his eyes carefully, seeing much there. Was amused.

Jessica touched Samone's shoulder. "Samone, I'm going to check on the pants."

"Okay, I'll be over in a sec." Samone watched her mother walk away, calculating distance, speed. The right moment she could resume conversation with Jon. And when the coast was clear, she started in on safe talk. Men's cologne.

"Kouros is a good one," she offered, pointing to the gray-and-blue-labeled bottle to his right.

"I've never tried it."

"You should . . . I love the stuff."

Jon nodded to the clerk, as if Samone's words were gold.

"Cash or charge?" the clerk asked, glad for a sale.

"Charge."

"Macy's? American Express?" he went on to say, details being everything.

"Macy's." Jon pulled out his wallet. It was black and slim. It took him a minute to find the burgundy credit card.

Samone pulled back from the counter, afraid of what he would say; the holiday heavy in the air.

"I better go. Have a good weekend." It was the only salutation she trusted.

"Yeah, you, too," Jon pitched, his voice level, not too concerned.

Across the sales floor, Jessica Lewis checked the seam on a pair of ramie cotton pants, saw how the thread gave, and knew they'd last only one season.

"Anything?" Samone had appeared so quickly that Jessica jumped.

"Girl, you scared me."

"Next time I'll put bells on my sneakers."

"You weren't over there long."

"He's just a co-worker."

"I'm not saying a word."

"Mom, please."

"Well, he may just be a co-worker, but that man had diamonds in his eyes when he saw you."

"Really, now."

"Really." Her sixth sense alerted, Jessica turned around quickly. Caught Jon staring. She stared back, her look no longer kind. Was about to tell Samone when he walked away.

Good, Jessica thought quickly, not ashamed.

Samone rinsed her sink, glad that the dishes were done and the counters were wiped. She'd take a nice warm shower, curl up on her sofa, let the TV watch her, and make it through Memorial Day Sunday night alone.

Would remember Memorial Day weekends past.

Barbecues. The music—wonderful; good food and the hot sun making everything more alive; Max getting her drinks, wiping sweat from her brow, slow jamming with her under a blanket of white stars; holding her in the quiet of early morning as they waited for a train or for the sun to rise.

She wondered what he was up to. Wondered if he too was sitting around thinking about what it used to be like.

Listening hard to the sound of the city moving

through her open windows, listening hard to all that life was about, Samone smiled half-mast, counted whatever blessings she considered herself having, and got into the shower.

The warm water fell upon her like summer rain. She closed her eyes and allowed it to run over her hair, against her lashes.

The phone rang. But through the rush of water, the soft tingling of electronic bells seemed too far away to be concerned with.

Could be anybody. Pat, her mother. Max . . . *If I'm that important, they'll call back.*

The next night, he did. . . .

"Whatcha doing?" was the question, touching some private, secret part of her. As if he knew she hadn't been doing a damn thing a second before he called.

"Watching TV."

His voice, still seductive, corralled her.

"Come see the fireworks."

"Where?" *But you know where, Samone. And you know why. . . .*

"Here. Come and watch them with me." It wasn't a question.

"Okay," she answered, up and off her couch.

Samone got dressed and called a cab. An easy thing to do. The day spent in Jersey at the family picnic had been a bust; everybody had a somebody but her. Two cousins wearing engagement rings, while a third was expecting her second child in two months.

No ease. No recluse. Aunts asking, "Where's

Max?'' as if Samone had killed him and buried him in the backyard. Even Sandra, her coolest of cousins, wasn't able to hold back the question.

A rough day finished when her uncle Chicken had dropped her off, Samone had been all too glad to get back home and escape her relatives' scrutiny. Her Memorial Day weekend had been seemingly a bust, until Jon called.

Going to his place was easy.

On the ride downtown, Samone reminded herself that she was going for the fireworks. But there were worse lies she had told.

Jon met her in the hall, both of them giddy as children.

''We'll ride up to the top floor and then take the stairs.''

''Where are we going?'' The sound of an exploding rocket rumbled down the elevator shaft.

''The roof.''

The night moved on, filled with the roar of rockets and exploding color bursts in the night sky. They drank champagne and oohed with the best of them, and then the fireworks were over and it was time to leave.

Jon had touched her there on the utility shack, high above city traffic. Had touched softly, with want, the rise of her lip and the slope of her chin. With careful fingers, he had traced her profile and disturbed the place where her hair met her shoulders.

Had stared deep into her eyes, never saying a word.

It was in this silence, as warm and potent as the night, that they squeezed into the crowded elevator and rode down seven floors, belly to belly.

With the same pervasive quiet, they walked to his front door and stepped inside. I came for the fireworks, she told herself as Jon put his arms around her. *The fireworks,* as her eyes closed to the sight of his lips moving in close. As a strong heat moved through her, and her lips parted to receive his. Fireworks, she considered right before Jon's phone started ringing and he moved away to answer.

Samone looked around her, the quiet now a different type of silence. Up the hall she heard Jon say, "Hello?" and knew it was Daryn on the other end.

Samone was spinning the world globe without interest when he returned. Ringing phones always meant bad news. Jon's was no different.

"That was Daryn," he announced, forcing himself to look at her even if she wouldn't return the favor.

"I'm sure. . . . It's all bullshit anyway, Jon. . . . Hell, I don't even know why I came."

" 'Cause you wanted to see the fireworks." He smiled, and Samone knew he was telling lies. For a long time she looked at him, refusing to hide how pissed off she was.

"What was I supposed to do?" Jon asked. "Tell her no?"

" 'Course not. She's the one you sleep with. It doesn't matter. I'm out of here."

"I didn't know she'd be back tonight. That's not my fault," was Jon's final defense as she stood at the elevator, giving it exactly three seconds to arrive before she would take the stairs.

The elevator door slid open, and Samone stepped in.

"You're wrong, Jon. It is your fault. I feel like some slut from 'cross town."

"If Daryn came and saw you here..." He couldn't finish the sentence.

"What, Jon? She'd know the truth. Like how you really feel about me. What you really want. That's why I'm here. Fireworks ain't got shit to do with it. You just wanted to fuck me."

"It's not like that."

"Oh, yeah. What's it like?"

"If that's the case, why did you come?"

"Because I was uptown, doing nothing, and you invited me over."

"Even though you knew all I wanted was to sleep with you."

Samone looked at him a long time. Gave up the truth. "Yes."

"So maybe I thought I could, is it a crime?"

"Is Daryn on her way? Forget it. Good-bye."

"Samone, wait."

Men always said that, told you "Wait," as if they'd had a change of their minds, their plans. Their hearts, last minute. Or had something you could really use if you gave them ten extra seconds of your time.

"Fuck you. Jon. Fuck. You."

The doors closed, and Samone was gone.

*   *   *

Coming home, and feeling less than zero, she glanced around, and the neatness of her apartment roused a smile from her. Samone closed the front door and gazed at the jade cat.

She had loved the large feline carved from stone the moment she had laid eyes on it. Max had put out a hefty sum for the pound of Oriental jade. Samone used to consider herself just like that cat: expensive, lustrous, special. Rare.

Living a lie? Have I been living some great lie and the folks around me bought into it? Did they wake up one day and discover that I was just fronting? That I was none of those things?

Jon . . . I keep saying "Not you." Keep saying that Max played me like a piano, but you wouldn't. But you've played this concerto with no real regard for me. . . . I needed for you to show me I mattered. More than Daryn, more than anything. That's what tonight was about, you showing me that you needed me, no matter how far and fast I'm running.

But you couldn't do it. Couldn't show me because it ain't so, is it. Thanks for the reality check. Thank you very much. . . .

Her phone rang. She thought not to answer. But the need to got the better of her.

"Hello?"

"Hey, girlfriend, where you been?" Pat asked.

"Nowhere special. . . . How was your day?" Samone said, refusing to tell any more of her secrets.

*   *   *

Time moved on. Samone and Jon still did lunch every now and then, but Jon's whole world was Daryn, and Samone grew weary of his happiness.

July fourth found Samone shut in with the flu. But Pat and her daughter, Shamika, kept Samone company, watching videos and eating takeout barbecue from Sherman's on 157th Street.

That holiday was different from the last. That holiday brought no calls to "come see the fireworks."

14

Just what she needed, or so it seemed. It had been so long since Samone had been dancing, she couldn't think of a reason not to. Besides, when was the last time she and Pat had hung out at a club? Dressed to the nines, sipping white wine, and laughing like schoolgirls at every jerk who tried to hit on them.

Still, they decided to call it an early night. Their behinds grew weary from sitting at the bar, and the DJ started playing hip-hop music, which they found offensive—too many references to bitches and ho's. Then there was the crowd; the stream of young people had been constant since a little after midnight.

"Young people." What a catch phrase. I used to be one of them myself, Samone thought glumly, letting her mind wonder all of ten seconds about what Jon and Daryn were doing. *The Nasty,* came a mean thought. Samone picked up her drink and sucked melted ice.

Pat yawned, looked at Samone with tired red eyes. "Damn, Samone, am I getting old or what?"

Samone nodded. "Must be the 'what.' " She laughed, tired and sleepy herself. It was *way* past her bedtime.

"What time is it?"

"Five minutes since the last time you asked. Why don't you go and call Ray and tell him we're on our way home."

"Yeah," Pat said, easing her latex-covered behind off the high bar stool. "Guess you're right. Even though the mister was very cool about me stepping out with you, I know for a fact he's sitting up in the living room with one eye on the clock and the other on the front door."

Samone moved her on. "Go on. I'll be here when you get back." She watched as Pat disappeared into the crowd.

Turned back and order one for the road.

The color of his jacket, red, was what caught her eye first. The smell of cologne was what caught her nose. The sound of his voice caught her ear. Samone couldn't help but look at the man who had taken Pat's chair without so much as asking.

"Courvoisier," he said, a ten snug between the middle and ring finger, gathered upward like an unfolded fan.

Samone wanted to look away, but he was the most scrumptious thing she had seen all night. His skin was the color of caramel, his lashes silky and long. The tapered waves ending above his ears was pure genes. Nothing made those waves in his head except his momma, his daddy, and God.

His close shave was still close, and the slope of his jaw was lionlike and sculptured. His voice, low timbred, had Max beat by an octave. A second before she was going to look away, he turned his head quick and caught her staring.

Gave a little move of his head, his way to say hello without actually speaking, and turned his attention back to the bartender making his drink.

Samone's heart beat. *One-night stand? I've never done that, but Lord knows this man next to me could make me.* Samone looked around, smiling for no one's benefit except her own.

His drink arrived, and she took a sip of hers.

Felt his eyes on her a long time, his gaze like cool fingers along her profile.

Samone realized she was holding her breath. Released it so soft and slow, it hurt. *Say something. Come on. Open up those lips and speak to me. 'Cause I ain't got a damn thing to say to you but yes.*

"Excuse me, that's my seat," Pat announced, arriving and not the least impressed by his looks, his smell, or the color of his jacket.

For a split second he sought Samone's face: *Last chance?* But the spell was broken by Pat's arrival. She looked away, the moment fading.

"Sure, no problem," he said, gathering his drink,

slipping away. His eyes were heavy on Samone's, full of *Maybe next time*.

"Damn, Pat, couldn't you have given me two more minutes?"

"What? Him? Come on, Samone. You know he wasn't nothing but a player."

"Maybe, but hell, I'd play for a night."

"Child, you have lost your mind."

Samone looked away. *Not my mind, Pat, just the man I think I love.*

"What do you think?"

Samone looked at the two bathing suits in Jon's hands. One was colorful and of the boxer variety, the other looked like something from Fredericks of Hollywood.

Jon was going on vacation and needed a bathing suit. Seven days in Cancún, just him and Daryn. "Send you a postcard," he'd promised Samone. But she didn't want a postcard. She didn't want him to go.

He held up the least risqué one. "This?"

"Yeah." It really didn't matter to her.

Samone was annoyed and hungry. She wanted out of the store. Wanted lunch.

"Two minutes," he said, dashing off to the dressing room.

Samone took a seat and looked at her watch. Jon's twenty minutes had turned into half an hour. It didn't make sense to her—waiting till the last minute to get a bathing suit? The more she thought about it, the more she realized that Jon had done this on purpose.

He wanted to rub in her face that he was going with somebody else; to remind her of what she had given up. But Samone knew exactly what she had given up.

Jon reappeared, shocking the hell out of her. The blue bikini fit him like nothing ever had. The only thing between him and nakedness was a few inches of material.

"What do you think?" he asked, standing sideways for her benefit.

"Whatever," Samone muttered, looking away.

On the streets; the lunch hour nearly up. Jon popped the last of his hot dog into his mouth, sipped the rest of his soda, and dumped the can into the garbage.

"Daryn's excited?" Samone found herself asking.

"Yeah. She's bringing like a ton of sunscreen, being a natural blonde and all."

Blonde? Samone hadn't known that. It was the first time Jon had mentioned anything about what Daryn looked like.

"In that case, she should."

Jon looked around him. "A whole week under that sun. God, I can't wait."

"So, what time's your flight?"

"Leaving out of La Guardia at five forty-six this evening."

"All packed?"

"Everything except my bathing suit."

"So," Samone began, hesitant to ask, unable not to, "when are you coming back?"

"Why? Are you going to miss me?" Jon was enjoying this.

"No. . . . Seriously, when are you coming back?"

"I'll be back in New York on Thursday night."

"Back to work on Friday?"

"No. I'm not coming in right away. Be back to work on Monday."

Jon stopped and leaned in close, his face inches from her own. Samone thought he was going to kiss her. Her eyes closed.

She couldn't breathe, waiting for his lips on hers. Waiting for him to tell her he'd changed his mind. That he still loved her. Felt a napkin on the side of her mouth and opened her eyes.

"Mustard," Jon said apologetically.

Sometimes you long for other lives, other faces. You look around you and decide that there were other places you'd rather see, other people you'd rather be. Today was one of those days; city living wasn't worth shit, being a manager meant less than zero, and a cotton skirt couldn't hold a candle to a bikini on a white sandy beach.

Samone took in the tall, tight buildings and the screaming after-work traffic and wished she were Dorothy. Wished she had heels that she could click to take her away from here.

New York City was in the midst of a heat wave. There had been a brown-out just the other night; for an hour Samone had lain in the dark, sweating and panting as her air conditioner struggled against low wattage to cool her.

Here into day three of the oppressive heat, Samone didn't think she could take another second of it. But even as she sought cool air, she knew the real problem was Jon. He had been avoiding her since he got back from Cancún.

She had called him that Monday; he couldn't do lunch. Same thing for Tuesday. They had set a lunch date for Wednesday, but he had backed out at the last minute.

Samone was stagnant. Had to get moving. There was only one way to do that. She had to talk to Jon. Whether he listened or not, she had to.

Samone sat on her couch. Got up. Took one last drag off her cigarette and contemplated another. Stared at the phone, wishing it gone. Wishing what she was about to do was done already.

I can do this. I can pick up the phone and do this. That's why God gave you a mouth, vocal cords, and a brain. So when you had to tell somebody something, you had everything you needed to speak. To open up your God-given mouth and say all those words you've been rehearsing all day.

Samone sat back down, swallowed. What she was going to say to Jon was set. The problem was, every time she thought about actually picking up the phone, her throat got tight.

And then there was that voice. That one that was

smug, high and mighty, and never had much use for a white man. The voice that coexisted within her. The one that told her, *He don't love you. He loves Daryn. Don't you know that? . . . What can you possibly do with a white man? What does he know about your world? . . . Daryn's the one he took to Cancún, not you. He doesn't care about you. . . . Besides, you know your momma and your daddy would have a fit . . . a white man? You must be crazy.*

Samone had loved in fear before and knew the perils. Determined not to repeat the same mistakes, she took a deep breath. It was time to let the fear go.

Samone didn't use the number often and could remember only the first two numbers. Just one more way to keep her distance. *Because if I knew his number by heart, then he would have been important.*

Samone didn't know if she wanted him in her life or simply wanted to get away for good. Either way, she would be free. Either way.

She nervously lit a cigarette, exhaled, and picked up the phone. All those reasons not to do this jumped her. Fear settled next to her, but she was too deep into it to stop what had begun. Her finger hit the first of seven numbers.

With the final number entered, there was a split second of nothing before Samone got the busy signal. She listened to it dimly, her mind elsewhere.

The easiest thing for her was to tell herself that at least she'd tried. That she should take his being on the phone with somebody else as a sign that said ''Don't do this.'' So for a while, she didn't.

She did other things. Channel surfed through the eighty stations that came with her cable service, picked up a magazine, only to put it down.

Went to the phone and hit redial. Jon's line was still busy.

Samone hung up and went to find clothes for tomorrow. The weatherman had forecasted another scorcher.

Two women wait, one blond, the other brunette. Each is oblivious of the other. Both wait for things needed. Both wait for the same thing but don't know it.

It is a quarter after five. Both have been waiting fifteen minutes. The office lobby is empty, save for an occasional worker and the cleaning man mopping the hard glossed floor as he whistles his own private melody. His voice is pitched and strong; he whistles without restraint.

The elevator comes and goes with a bing! *each time it departs or arrives. An occasional passenger gets off, None of whom the women wait for.*

The brunette pulls out a cigarette and lights it cautiously. It is the sound of the match striking paper that causes the blonde to turn her head.

She wears her nervousness like a banner, for all to see.

"Can I have one?" she asks.

The brunette nods. Gives her one. Steadies her cigarette to light the other. They both inhale and exhale, gray smoke moving around them.

The blonde steps back and away, their brief bond broken.

The elevators arrive one after the other. No one gets off or on. The cleaning man continues his melody; it moves with the flow of his long jute mop.

The brunette eyes the large clock on the marble wall. Wonders if she missed him.

The blonde looks at her watch, wondering if he left already.

The cleaning man dips the mop in water and wrings it with a strong, steady grip. It lands on the floor with a flop! *and he picks up his melody again. He is content in who he is and what he does.*

An elevator arrives with a bing! *It is the sound of leather soles on the hard floor that brings both women to attention. Even before he rounds the slight corner, they know it is him.*

Both move forward. Both have words ready on their tongue. It isn't until they are halfway there that they realize they are waiting for the same man. In a millisecond, they know this without a single word. Neither will surrender. Ultimately it will be Jon's choice.

"Samone? Daryn? What's going on?"

"I was waiting for you," Daryn said, moving one step forward. Samone remained behind.

"I thought we got everything straight last night."

"It's not that simple, Jon. Can we go somewhere and talk?"

Immediately his eyes went to Samone, but her face

was masked, revealing nothing. Samone nodded. Did not smile.

"Go. We'll talk later," she told him, turning and walking away. Daryn's words were still crystal clear in her head. *It's not that simple, Jon.*

Samone knew Daryn was right.

Samone didn't feel like television. She didn't need pictures, she had personal visions of her own. It had been a long time since she had done this for herself. Every once in a while life demanded that she did.

So she went through her albums, picked out a handful, sat in front of her stereo, played her records. Sang along.

She played Luther Vandross and Bebe & CeCe Winans. Sang along with Joni Mitchell and Phoebe Snow. Was so into her solo, she did not hear the doorbell ring the first time.

It rang again, and with utmost reluctance, she went to the intercom.

"Yes?"

"It's Jon. Can I come up?"

"Okay."

How did I know you'd be here? How did I know that you were at a point in your life where nothing was going to keep you away? How did it come to be that we arrived at the same place at the same time, for once?

His face was full of apology. But there was nothing to apologize for. Samone gathered him into her arms, a homecoming long overdue.

Her fingers found themselves in his hair, absently stroking the softness, the straightness. Touching his face, the white skin; these things—"skin" and "hair"—denying her the right to be loved for far too long. Made the enemy not by choice, but by tradition. In his arms, feeling the warmth of his heart beating fast and steady, Samone knew it would never matter again; would never be cause to keep her away from him.

With no desire to let go, Samone held him for a long time. There had been a hundred things Jon was ready to speak when she opened the door, but her embrace quieted them all. Without a word she released him and closed the door. Smiled and said, "I was having one of my miniconcerts. You caught me in the middle."

He followed her to the living room. In the ashtray a cigarette had nearly burned itself out. Six albums lay about the floor. An empty glass rested against a speaker.

"I'm sorry about Daryn."

"You don't have to be. You and Daryn had nothing to do with me." It was a lie, but the mood dictated that she say it.

"I never expected to see both of you there waiting."

Samone got back on the floor, comfortable in the intimacy she had created for herself. "I didn't know who she was. She even bummed a smoke."

"It was over before it started."

Samone nodded. "Yeah, I know."

"Then I guess I don't have to explain why it happened."

"No. I know why it happened."

Jon laughed, and a quick, funny thought fell from his lips. "It's a long way to Tipperary."

She looked at him with bright, startling eyes. "A long way to me, you mean."

"To us," he offered, searching her face.

She nodded. Smiled. Became the hostess.

"Want something to drink?"

"No. I just came from a bar. That's where we went to talk."

"Well, I'm going to get a refill. Be back."

In her absence, Jon noticed that faint shading of rectangles on the walls. Knew pictures that hung there a long time had been removed. He didn't have to take the thought far to know of whom.

Samone came back, sat on the floor, and took a long sip of her soda. She faced Jon, her face serious.

"I tried to call you last night . . . I realized that nothing would change for me until I talked to you."

"I was on the phone with Daryn."

"So I gathered. So where does that leave us, Jon? Are we supposed to be like lovers now or something?" She let loose a nervous laugh. "I'm not sure what's supposed to happen next."

"Does it matter?"

"What?"

"If we sleep together or not?"

"Well, we slept together before."

"I'm talking about now."

"What you don't seem to understand, Jon, that where I'm standing, it's a whole 'nother place. Racism is alive and well in America. Nobody can't tell me it's not. And while it's been a long time since anybody called me nigga, to a lot of white people I still am. So when I look at you, sometimes all I see is your whiteness. Do you understand?"

"Samone, I've always understood that. But that's not how I see you."

"Really. Well, what do you see?"

"I see this incredibly fine attractive woman who's stolen my heart."

"Cut the bullshit, Jon. What do you see?"

"I see Samone."

"Who am I? Who am I to you?"

"You're somebody I really really like."

"See, you can't even say it."

"Say what?"

"That I'm black . . . it's number one with me. Beyond being female, I'm black first. You have to look at me and say to yourself that Samone is a black woman. That her world is not like mine. That no matter how we share, it will always be different for her. That's what you have to realize."

"It wasn't a big deal for Yvonne."

"I'm not Yvonne. I am Samone, black and female. This is what defines me. Not my fancy clothes or the way I talk."

"So what are you saying?"

"I'm saying that if you want to do this, want to be with me, then you have to remember who I am. Yes,

I know love knows no color, but the world sure does. And every time I hear about a Yusef Hawkins or a Joseph Pannell, I want to run out into the streets and kill the first white mutherfucker I see, just to let them know how it feels. And that might be you, do you understand? . . . There's a part of me that wants you, but there's a part of me that can hate you real easy. That's not your fault . . . but that's how I feel.''

Samone sat back, her words spent, the rush gone. She looked at him, seeking to affirm that he understood. He returned her gaze. *He still doesn't get it.*

''Samone, you think I don't know what's going on out there? Of course I do, but for you to blame me and hold me responsible, that's crazy. I haven't got shit to do with any of it.''

''And you want to know something, Jon? As long as you look at it that way, nothing's going to change.''

''What do you want me to do? Hang a banner out of my window telling white people to start treating black people better?''

''Yes. If that's what it will take.''

''You can't put that on my shoulders. My name is Jonathon Everette. I don't own the world, I just live in it.''

''That's a fucking cop-out.''

''It may be. But I don't know what else to say.''

''That's the problem. You really don't.''

He reached over and took her hands. The contrast in skin color was abrupt. ''Look, Samone. I'm here because I want to be with you. For over a year I've been trying to tell you, and maybe you're finally listening. But don't expect me to be a poster boy for social change. That's not why I'm here.''

Samone pulled her hands away. ''Then maybe you should leave.''

''Don't do this. Don't throw up another wall to me.''

''But you don't understand, Jon.''

''I understand.''

''No. You don't. . . . Someday somebody is going to say something when we're together. Ten times out of ten, the remark will be against me. And if you don't understand the point I'm trying to make, how are you going to understand?''

''When you were going for that abortion, did I know anything about being pregnant?''

''No.''

''Is me in your life more important than what people will say? That's the bottom line, Samone. And that's what you have to decide. *You* have to decide if you're willing to be with me, 'cause I've already decided.''

''It's not that easy, Jon.''

''I never said it was.''

The day became too long, and a weariness overcame her. Samone didn't want to talk anymore. She just wanted to give in to the exhaustion. She did not want to talk about race, creed, color, America, white, black, or racism. She wanted ease.

Comfort.

Jon was on the floor beside her before she had time

to consider. He took her into his arms. Held her for a long time. For a minute, Samone didn't need another thing. This was how it was with him, these moments, where everything was wonderful and complete and she didn't want for anything. So she took the comfort he offered and opened herself up to all the things her heart was hearing. But it became too overwhelming, and she retreated.

She went to her stereo and put on a record. Lit a cigarette and closed her eyes. When she opened them, a part of her expected Jon to be gone. But he was still there, watching her. Watching and waiting for her mind to be made up.

"Still here?" The bitterness in her voice surprised neither of them.

"Do you want me to go?" His eyes were shiny, borderline tears. Jon was hurting, and she knew it. Samone longed to look away from him but couldn't. Shook her head in sad defeat.

"I can't do this."

"So your mind's made up?"

She cast him a leery glance, said, "Is it?" snickered, and looked away.

This was the Samone that scared him. The one that was cold and indifferent. The Samone full of rage, who could hate him without question or pause. But they were almost there, and nothing in Jon could stop him from trying. He pressed on, knowing the precipice she now dangled from.

"You're scared, Samone. And that's okay. It's okay to be scared. Relationships are very scary; that's one of the reasons people aren't in them for very long. But it's about what you think you need most: me here or me gone."

Samone closed her eyes again and sighed. The sound was like a sudden rustle of leaves in the wind, full of consolation and tenderness.

She looked at him. "Do you know how I feel about you? I mean, beyond my fears."

"And your anger."

She looked surprised, having not considered that part of it. "Yes. That too. I mean, you come off like some damn Prince Charming. All you need is a white horse. But you're not. You're not perfect, and I know that. And it's like being with you would be buying into the myth that white is right. And while I know you're not a ruler, you still belong to the club."

"You make it sound like I belong to the KKK."

"I know you don't. But there's something I don't trust. Like, why me? What is it about me that you need so?"

"Why are people attracted to whom they're attracted to? What was it about Max that made you want him?"

She smiled. "He was tall, dark, and handsome."

"I rest my case."

"Come on, Jon. I'm neither handsome nor tall."

"You have a fierceness about you and a protectiveness about you that's captivating. Something I don't have."

"That's because life's done you different. You don't acquire what you don't need."

"Maybe."

"That goes back to what I was saying about where I'm coming from and where you're standing."

"Is that my fault?" Jon asked, sensing her softer demeanor.

"No."

"And all this time you thought I was after your body."

"Oh, like you aren't."

"You want a lie or the truth?"

"Don't bother about answering. I know the answer."

"You see, Samone? I told you it wouldn't be so bad."

"What's that?"

But he never answered, just smiled. Samone didn't need a road map. She knew where they were heading.

The writing was on the wall.

15

No other man would. No other man had. But here it was Saturday afternoon, and there Jon sat, flipping through a magazine.

The woman who came into Dina's Beauty World had taken a long hard second look. Nobody could ever remember seeing a white man sitting in Dina's on a hot Saturday afternoon. Dina herself couldn't recall a white man in her shop, waiting for his woman to get a touch-up. But there he was, not even sweating, even though it was close to eighty inside.

Most of the women didn't know whom he was waiting for, and those who did took turns looking over Samone and then looking back at Jon, trying to decipher just what it all meant and how it had come to be. Their minds moved faster than a main-drive computer as they tried to decide if it was good, bad, or just plain none of their business.

Jon was there because Saturday was their day together and Samone had to get a touch-up. He was curious about the ritual she went through every six weeks like clockwork. She had sent him out once for sodas, and if Dina didn't take the dryer off her head soon, she was going to send him out again.

Watching with cryptic fascination, Jon saw creme relaxers and smoking hot combs turn thick tight hair straight; watched the amazing things beauticians did with hair weaves.

And the women. Once they sat in that chair, they didn't move, squirm, or hardly blink. Sometimes they talked, but mostly they were silent, as if they could make the beautician give them the perfect hairstyle if they concentrated hard enough.

Jon had never seen such a thing in his life. He'd never realized the power of those who wielded the comb and the hot curler. No wonder some men did hair for a living.

Samone lifted the beehive-shaped cylinder from her head and leaned forward. "Dina, how much longer?"

"Five more minutes. We want your wrap to be nice and dry."

Wrap. Jon never knew that women "wrapped" their hair. When Samone told him she was getting a wrap, he thought Dina was going to wrap her hair in cellophane, but once again he got an education.

Dina had put white creme on Samone's head, making her sit until her eyes starting to tear; then she was taken to the wash bay and was shampooed a few times. Then Dina sent her back under the dryer, where Samone had to sit for fifteen minutes. When she got up, her hair looked stiff as a board. She invited Jon to touch it. It *was* stiff as a board.

Then it was back to the sink for another rinse, then into the chair. That's when Dina started combing Samone's hair around her head. For ten minutes Dina worked the comb until all of Samone's hair was literally "wrapped" around her head, tight and neat.

Then it was back under the dryer, where she had been for the last twenty-five minutes.

Twenty minutes after that, Samone and Jon were on the street. Her hair moved with the simplest of breeze.

"Whatcha think?"

"That's a *wrap*."

"You're so damn silly."

"That's what you love about me best."

"Absolutely," Samone said, taking his arm. "Absolutely."

Samone spotted Akeem before he spotted her. Even though he lived in her neighborhood, she hadn't seen him since last fall. Their meetings were always intense and warm, his concern centering on her and how life was treating her. He had stopped inviting her to his mosque years ago, accepting the fact that Muslim life would never be Samone's thing.

Samone and Akeem had grown up together on the same block in Harlem, back in the days when he was still known as Kevin. When Samone was running around in ponytails and knee-high socks, Kevin/ Akeem was never too far out of her sight. He had moved through her childhood like a sudden breeze, arriving without warning.

He still walked with that hesitant gait, which was why Samone knew it was him half a block away.

She braced herself.

Samone had known Kevin/Akeem when he was a well-kept, soft-spoken little boy with a serious love crush on her. Had known him as the first boy she'd ever kissed, at the age of ten, when a group of her friends decided it was time to find out what kissing a boy was like.

Samone remembered the smell of onions that clung to him and how the setting sun tinted the tips of his hair earthy beige. Samone remembered his spindly ashy legs and how she stopped breathing as she moved to try this new thing—kissing boys.

Samone remembered those lips that had tasted salty, warm, rubbery, and dry. Her first kiss—quick, brief, and without emotion. Still, she remembered a kind of thrill that had raced through her and how Kevin/Akeem always looked at her sideways, as if he knew a secret after that.

Samone had known Akeem when he was Kevin, before the change of his name and religion. She had known him as a little boy in love with her. Kevin/ Akeem had carried her books home from junior high and even tongue-kissed her in the park after dark.

Now, as he drew closer, she could only wonder what he thought of the white man beside her.

"How have you been, Sister?"

As she sought an appropriate response, Samone sensed what she always did whenever Akeem was in her presence—bitterness and longing. For a moment, she felt the need to test those lips, no longer the color of summer peaches, to see if they were still rubbery, still dry. Still warm. She thought, in that split second, that if she kissed Akeem who used to be Kevin, he would see the love Jon had reborn deep inside of her and would understand her choice.

"I've been just fine," Samone replied. She turned to Jon. "This is my lover, Jon . . . Jon, this is Akeem."

And there on the street, half a block from her apartment, the two men shook hands, past and present coming together.

And damned if the whole thing wasn't A-okay with her.

"Jon?"

"Hum?"

"You awake?"

"No."

"You have to be, how else could you answer me?"

Jon sat up, the sheet gathering in a bunch at his waist, his skin glimmering in the darkness.

"What's wrong?"

"I was just thinking about today."

"Yeah."

"Yeah. I mean, we spent the whole day uptown and it was like okay."

"What did you expect?"

Samone looked off; after a long time, shrugged. "I don't know."

"The worst." He touched her shoulder with cool fingers. "You were expecting stones to be thrown at us and people calling you names."

"No, not exactly."

He caressed her hair. "Close, though."

"Yeah."

"So what does it mean?" Jon asked, his fingers trailing the ridge of her collarbone.

She swallowed audibly, seduced. "What does what mean?"

"Today. What happened. What *didn't.*"

"I don't understand."

"You do."

"I guess it means it's all right."

His fingers moved across her belly. "What's all right?"

"Us."

The tip of his finger touched her clitoris.

She moaned. Rolled toward him.

"And?"

And . . . Lord knows I love you, she thought, mute in his gentleness.

Beyond the grassy knolls and large oak trees, beyond the park benches and the black wrought-iron fence, the Hudson River glimmered as tiny tugs pulled freighters across the swirling water.

Riverside Park, an enclave for uptown residents, was in all its summer splendor as Samone and Pat indulged themselves this special time together.

Pat put the lid on the potato salad and handed Samone a napkin. "We haven't done this in a while," she said, moving swiftly with the knowledge that the impromptu picnic was full of news.

"Yeah, I've been busy lately."

"Don't I know it. Okay, who is he?"

Samone bit into the chicken leg. It was golden, crispy, and good to the tongue.

"Jon." She scooped up a bit of salad. The tomato slice fell off her fork, across her thigh, and onto the blanket.

"Jon? As in white boy Jon?"

"White man, Pat."

"So you went ahead and did it."

"Guess I did."

"Never thought I'd see the day."

Samone smiled tightly, her lips determined to hide her teeth. "Me neither."

"How long?"

"Just over a week."

"Not long."

"No."

They both looked toward the river.

A breeze rustled the trees. Sunlight dappled. A child laughed from far away.

Samone opened her mouth, knowing Pat would not. "He's a nice guy. He really is."

"I'm sure he is."

"No, I mean he really is, Pat."

"Yeah. I believe you."

"I want you to meet him."

"Okay."

"Will you say something?"

"What do you want me to say, Samone? Personally, a white man would never be my choice, but I can't tell you who you should be seeing. I tried that with Max, remember? Don't expect me to say you're making a mistake. I'm not gonna do that. Only you know if it's right or not."

Samone looked off, her eyes picking out Pat's daughter, Shamika, roller-skating on the cement walkway.

"Most of the time I think it's okay."

"It's them other times that's kicking your butt, right?"

"Something like that."

"He's making you happy?"

"Yeah."

"Then fine. He make you happy, I'm happy. He start acting up, well, that's another story."

"So, it's okay with you?"

"How long you been my best friend?"

"Since high school."

"You think I'm gonna let some man put an end to that?"

" 'Course not."

"All right, then. It's your life, Samone. You live it the way you think is best."

"This can't be Pat speaking."

"Who else is it?"

"You're so calm about it."

"Samone, you chose that man to tell your secret to. I knew sooner or later something was gonna happen."

"Looks like now is the time."

"Looks like it is."

"I haven't told my mother."

"Ask me if I'm surprised."

"What do you think she'll say?"

"Knowing Jessica? A whole lot."

"Pat, it's not a crime."

"Nobody ever said it was."

"So why do I feel so afraid?"

" 'Cause he's white and male." While there was a host of things Pat could have said on the subject, she knew her best friend really didn't want to hear them. Pat moved on.

"Listen, you know Shamika's party is coming up."

"When?"

"Three Saturdays from now. Fourish. But seeing as though you are her godmother, you can come early and help out."

"Figured that."

"And so you can't say I didn't tell you, Max will be there, and he's bringing somebody and her little girl."

"Max?"

"Yeah. I've met his new friend. She's nice enough. Name's Carol-Anne, can you get over that one? Well, I guess 'Carol-Anne' beats 'Zen' any day."

"I knew I'd run into him sooner or later."

"If you don't want to come, I'll understand, but I don't think Shamika will."

"Of course I'll be there."

"Bring Jonathon, if you want."

"You can call him Jon."

"Whatever. And in case you can't figure out what your goddaughter wants, she's been dying for a Fisher-Price kitchen, with all the accessories. Her mommy and daddy already laid out money on a computer, a bike, and party favors, ice-cream cake, and decorations."

"Is that supposed to be a hint, Patricia?"

"Well, it's definitely something."

"How much is this kitchen?"

"About seventy dollars."

"Seventy dollars? I could buy me a nice pair of pumps."

"Yeah, and on sale, I could get me two. But that's what she wanted, Auntie Samone."

"Well, only because she's my only goddaughter."

"Whatever the reason is good enough for me."

Samone switched back to her real concern. "So, it's okay?"

"You and Jon? How many times you gonna ask me?"

"Until I think you're telling the truth."

"Well, it's not who I'd pick for you. But Sam,

you're grown and on your own. You're too old to be told what to do.''

"Okay, I'll shut up. Give me a slice of that pie.''

"TV watching you?''

Jon smiled, half-asleep, the receiver nestled against his ear. He sat up, gingerly rubbing his eyes. Samone had been right.

Bare toed and in faded Levi's, Jon had settled into his recliner, remote control in one hand, a Bud in the other, and had flipped channels till he found the base-ball game.

Jon laughed. "Lucky guess.''

"But a correct one.'' The day, a gentle thing, had given birth to the evening soft about her.

This is what I've missed. Coming home from some-where and getting on the phone, hearing him missing me without him saying a word. Samone rolled onto her back, comfort nestling her.

"So how was the picnic?''

"Really nice. A nice day, good food. Me and Pat talked . . . I told her about you. Said she wasn't sur-prised.''

"Guess it's official.''

"Yeah, I guess it is.''

Spoken out loud, the word became truth.

Jessica Lewis slid softly off the Naugahyde stool and moved toward the Kenmore refrigerator. Behind her, late afternoon sun dusted the breakfast nook and a slice of polished tile floor. It turned the leaves of her spider plant white and made Samone softer in its shadows.

Samone sipped gingerly from her glass of Heineken, watching the smoke that curled aimlessly from two cigarettes laid lit and undisturbed in the crystal ashtray. Jessica Lewis gathered three ice cubes into her palm, glad for the coldness.

"I think I'm the only person in the world who puts ice in their beer."

It was an apology. Jessica suddenly found herself at fault for all that her daughter had become.

Samone carefully put the glass on the beige cork coaster and lowered her head. Sighed.

"Mom, it's not the worst thing. Is it?"

Jessica closed the fridge, the three ice cubes sticking to one another wetting her palms. Her sneakered feet made no sound as she moved back to the stool and used a leg to hoist her hip up on the padded seat.

There were worse things. And there were also better. There were things taken for granted; things assumed. Just an hour ago, as Jessica planted marigolds in her backyard, she had thought that life had been pretty good to her. That she and Odell had done well. Had raised a baby girl now grown, on her own and doing the right things. That at thirty-five, Samone had marked the milestone of going from a daughter to a good friend. That Samone could now speak on the level Jessica had been since Samone was born.

Just an hour ago, when the summer day had bought lots of sunshine and a warmth that prickled and soothed bare arms, she felt assured that she and Odell had conquered life and its varied responsibilities. That the seeds planted decades ago had blossomed like the tulips and the peach tree in their backyard.

Yes, there were worse things. But God forgive her, there would always be better.

"He's white," was what Jessica finally managed, her left foot searching and finding a resting place on the second rung of the stool.

"Don't you think I know that?"

"Have you thought about this? I mean, really thought about this? . . . Honey, white people are still killing black folks for being in Bensonhurst. For daring to have a flat in Howard Beach. For stopping for a damn bagel in Gravesend. Being black is all the reason white people need."

"Mom, I read the papers."

"Then you know what kind of world we're living in."

"But that doesn't matter to him."

"Yes, but it does to you."

Samone looked at her mother. Was hurt to see tears in those brown eyes. Jessica Lewis was more than concerned: she was afraid.

"Yes, it matters. And it's something I live with every time he calls or takes me out. Every time he rides the D train uptown, with or without me. Yes, it matters. But what he is is more to me than my fears."

"What is he to you, Samone?" Jessica dared with a look. But she looked away, already knowing the answer. Knowing from the moment Samone spoke his name and revealed the color of his skin.

''He's the one I want to be with.''

''You tell your daddy,'' Jessica said, thinking that what lay up the road and around the bend for everyone was anybody's guess.

''Okay.''

For a long time, it was quiet on the ride from Jersey to Harlem. Odell Lewis didn't even put on the radio. Every now and then Samone looked at her father and saw a strong black man humbled by his daughter's heart.

''Don't pass judgment till you meet him,'' Samone said, her back stiff and straight against the car seat, her hands in her lap. They itched to touch his broad shoulder. To soothe the knot from his brow.

''Won't change his color if I do.''

''Daddy, you raised me better than that. You were always going on about how the only way the world was going to survive was if we all got together. That's what you used to tell me whenever I ran off to the Black Panther Party rallies.''

''I was trying to protect you.''

''Like you're trying to protect me now. You can't. Nobody can. If it's a mistake, I'll know soon enough. But don't treat me like this. Like I done committed murder.''

''You gonna marry him?''

''Marry him? Daddy, we just started dating.''

''You thought about it.''

''No.''

"Your great-grandfather was lynched, and your great-great-grandfather was a slave."

"And so I'm supposed to hold Jon responsible?"

"If the shoe fits."

"How many times have I messed up in my life?"

"None, far as I know. But you and your momma keep secrets."

"Right. None. I don't do drugs. I work. I been supporting myself for a long time now. I'm over thirty. Don't you think I know a little about what's good for me?"

"Since when a white man been good for you?"

"It's not a 'white man,' it's Jon. Jonathon Everette."

"Samone, you know I never tried to interfere in your life. But baby, I just want you to know what you're getting into."

"Will you meet him, Daddy? Meet him and not prejudge before you do?"

"I don't have to meet him. I know what he is."

Tears gathered in her eyes. She wanted to tell her daddy that he was all wrong about Jon. But she could not find her tongue. So it went unsaid.

She called Jon as soon as she got in.

"It was awful."

"That bad, huh?"

"My mother cried. And my father talked about slavery and lynching. It ain't got shit to do with you."

"I'm coming over."

"No. Don't."

But they both knew he would.

It was her spot, Jon realized. There on the floor, by the stereo. It was her own private court, he realized, too. Where the ashtray, lighter, and cigarettes were her attendants, and visitors were not allowed to trespass.

She was laughing now, at something funny he had said. But he knew the sadness was just waiting in the wings for a curtain call.

"I don't know anything about you," Samone realized, stubbing out a cigarette and in need of another. But she had had too many already.

She stared at the discarded butts in the ashtray. "I'm gonna quit these things. They're gonna kill me."

Jon laughed. "Yeah, nothing like nicotine-flavored kisses. Especially first thing in the morning."

She studied him from the floor, her eyes sharp focused on him. "I don't know anything about you. I know you're from Malibu, and you have a brother. That's all. I don't know anything about your parents. Your friends. Nothing."

"Not much to tell."

"You know my whole life. How come you never shared yours with me?"

"I guess because it isn't all that great. Me and my brother were raised by an aunt and uncle. They were okay, but not really parents. They kept us clothed, fed, and in line, but they kept away, like they were afraid of getting too close. Later on I figured maybe if they had tried to love us and had succeeded, they might have been tempted to tell us the whole story. Of how my father's drug problem had figured in the state of California wanting to take us away. And that my aunt and uncle had decided to adopt us rather than to see us go into foster care.

"It's funny, but I can't remember ever seeing my father high, or shooting up. I remember him being real mellow and laid-back, that's all. But then again, I only knew my parents for a little while."

"What happened to them?"

"Let's just say they're gone."

"You can tell me, Jon."

"They gave custody to my aunt and uncle and split. My aunt knew that when my parents left for the 'movies' that they were not coming back."

"They just like left you at your aunt's?"

"Yeah, guess you could say that."

"How old were you?"

"I was eight. My brother was ten. I think that's why I wanted to come to New York and live. My mother's from New York. We visited one summer, stayed with some friends of hers. My mother was sort of the free spirit type. She painted watercolors and did great things with clay, but mothering wasn't her bag.

"My father was a musician. Played the bass. I remember our house always filled with music. A lot of jazz. I remember being in my room and hearing people like Stan Getz and Miles Davis late at night. My father loved Miles . . . from what I can piece together, he started doing heroin in the fifties 'cause it was considered the cool thing to do if you were a serious musician.

"To this day my brother won't even take a drink. He's afraid that he'll end up a real druggie and then his kid will be taken away. . . . I know it doesn't make real sense, but it does to him. . . . But enough of this talk. That was then."

"I'm sorry, Jon. I had no idea."

"I hardly tell anyone."

Samone watched him, weighing the burden of her next question and if he could stand to answer it. Or even if he wanted to.

"You never tried to find them?"

Jon looked off. His eyes glistened, caught in the light. Tears hovered, refusing to be released.

"Oh, I found them. Turned out they settled in Nevada. One state away. A whole lifetime of wondering, and they like were right next door . . . spent a lot of money and a lot of time looking for them. Couldn't believe it when I got the call . . . they were both dead. Had been dead a little over two years by then. Me and my brother took the flight to Nevada. Visited their graves. Cried.

"It was very bad. My brother never forgave me for that." He tapped his fingers against his chest. "But I had to know . . . in my heart, I had to. Till this day, my brother won't talk about it, which is really hard because sometimes I want to. I don't, though."

He looked up at her. His eyes, beacons of sorrow, drew her into their depths.

"It's hard, y'know?" He blinked, gathering unshed tears.

"I can imagine." But she really couldn't. She tried to imagine Jessica and Odell just going away and never coming back for her. *How could his parents look into his little face, those eyes, and just go away? How could they do that to him?*

"You said your mother was from New York. Didn't she have family?"

"Probably."

"You never tried to find any?"

Jon sighed. "A part of me wants to and a part of me doesn't. I mean, are my grandparents still alive? Aunts, uncles? I could be living right next door to a relative. But I'm afraid to look anymore. It took so long to find my parents, and the thought of finding more dead people . . . I just can't."

Samone knew it was painful, but she sensed he needed to speak it out loud.

"Why?"

"Why? They never came looking for me. They had to know about us, me and Jim. I mean, when my mother died, they had to know. But they never contacted us. My aunt and uncle never said a word. Like it didn't matter. So I say an eye for an eye. . . . I don't want to talk about this anymore."

But Samone wouldn't let it go.

"Did Yvonne know?" The sound of her name

seemed out of place in her living room. Out of place in her life.

Jon looked away. "No. I never told her."

Silence moved in, pain and despair heavy in the air. Samone's eyes were wide with regret.

"Thanks for sharing it with me. I know it wasn't easy."

Jon hadn't meant to burden her. He forced himself past his pain. "*De nada.* You're feeling better?"

Samone nodded, getting to her feet. "I want to play something for you, okay?"

"Okay."

Jon leaned back, his old wounds reopened, never quite healed.

"It's an old song. You probably don't know it."

"Who's it by?"

"No questions. Just listen."

Patti LaBelle's voice filled the air, "Come What May" speaking about wishes and longing, a banquet of dreams offered from one heart to the other. The song ushered the desires of the heart, wanting to give all that it could even if the reality was not so assured. That regardless of what happened, the love would be free of fear.

The song finished. Jon nodded. Closed his eyes and said, "Thank you."

"You're welcome." Samone extended her hand, a giving smile on her lips. "Come on, let's go to bed."

For a long time they just held each other, their minds unwilling to move past things come and gone.

And then Jon kissed her and Samone kissed him back, laughing against the darkness.

"Oh, Samone." He moved her into a tight embrace. His body trembled, a desperation moving through him as his mouth sought her breast. Samone understood the urgency of his hands over her body and was thankful for his tenderness in the heat of the moment.

And then he was coming fast, hard, and without her. Coming lightning quick deep, deep inside of her, her name his mantra, said over and over again, until the need to breathe took hold.

"I love you," he whispered in the aftermath.

"I know," she replied, her voice fragile and laid bare.

16

"Auntie Samone!"

"Hi, baby. My, don't we look pretty."

With a lace pink dress, pink barrettes dangling from the end of twelve fluffy braids, and pink lace-trimmed socks, Shamika was pretty in pink for her seventh birthday party.

In celebration of this milestone reached, Pat had bought Shamika her first pair of strapless black patent-leather shoes with a half-inch heel. While it was a far cry from her mother's pumps, they made Shamika feel very grown-up.

"Where's Mommy?"

"She ran down to the store. She forgot to get ice."

"Where's Daddy?"

"Getting dressed."

White and pink helium balloons floated up against

the high ceiling. Streamers ran down the hall into the living room, gathering as a canopy over a huge white cake topped with real strawberries.

Pat and Ray had pulled out all the stops.

"So, you're the birthday girl, huh?"

"Yep. I'm seven!"

"You are?"

"Yep! And you know what Uncle Max got me?"

"No, honey, what?"

"He got me three dresses, a pair of roller skates, and a five-hundred-dollar savings barn."

"That's *bond,* baby. Savings bond."

Samone looked up. And there he was. How long he had been standing there, she wasn't sure. But she sensed he had been there a while.

Max had watched her as she came through the door, her peach shorts and white T-shirt agreeing with the burnished glow summer gave her. Agreeing with her hair gathered and the dark sunglasses removed upon seeing Shamika. Agreeing with the shiny gold chain about her wrist and the seductive one that circled her ankle.

Love had done Samone well this summer. She glowed.

His absence had not diminished her in the least bit. Samone looked as good as the last time Max had seen her.

She smiled, telling her heart to still itself. Spoke her words carefully. "Hello, Max. Did Pat coerce you into coming early to help, too?"

"No. Actually, I got here early on purpose."

"Oh? And why's that?"

"Because I wanted to talk to you."

"About what?"

"Just catch up. See how you are doing. Tell you how I'm doing, et cetera."

Swift as a panther, Samone brought him face-to-face with who she was these days.

"Well, I'm just fine. Life is treating me right, and I have no complaints." She gave him the once-over. "You seem to be doing all right."

Max laughed, Samone's scathing tongue welcomed. "Let's blow up some balloons."

Samone looked up at the ceiling. "Balloons? Doesn't she have enough?" *It's really okay, isn't it? Me and him living different, separate lives. I can look at him and not long for anything more than what I got.*

"Just a few more. Pat got a helium tank, so it'll be easy."

"Well, let me put my bag down. And how did Shamika find out what you got her for her birthday? Wasn't it supposed to be a surprise?"

Max laughed. "You seen my baby. How could her uncle Max not tell her what was in those packages?"

"Yeah. She does look like a little doll."

Everybody wanted a little girl to adorn in ribbons and bows, to have people tell you how pretty she is. . . . Samone pushed the thought away.

She had a new life now.

Max, wearing his eagerness like he wore his fitted

cotton shirt, wasted no time getting into Samone's business.

"I hear you're seeing somebody."

Samone grabbed a balloon. "Oh, I'm sure you have."

She slipped it onto the tip of the helium tank. That was as far as she got. She didn't know a damn thing about helium tanks and wasn't about to take any chances. Max moved to help, and their arms touched in surprise contact. Samone stepped back as if burned. Max pretended not to notice.

"You get the ribbon. I'll put in the air."

Samone plucked up a white ribbon and spoke what she knew she would have to this day.

"He's white and we're happy."

"Well, if you're happy, then Lord knows I'm happy for you, Samone."

She risked a look into those Chinaman's eyes. Saw their life together moving through them. They lassoed her but soon let her go.

Max was always a gentleman. Samone let go a tiny laugh.

"I'm seeing someone, too. I'm sure you heard."

Samone nodded. This "talk" expected.

"She's a little older than me. Has a daughter about eight, and she's good people. I'm happy."

"We'll, I'm happy you're happy." Samone meant it and was glad the discussion was over. Enough of this; there was a party to be had.

But Max wasn't quite finished. "I'll always love you."

It was a statement that Samone thought epitomized most men's stupidity. Like they leave you just to go on loving you. Made better sense to just stay around. But that was Max's problem now, not hers. It no longer mattered.

"I know. But what the hell, right?"

Max agreed, "What the hell."

Above them, balloons danced against the ceiling.

"Maybe we should do like five more. I swear any more, and we'll have a fire hazard."

"Still smoking?"

"Is my ass black?"

"Same old Samone."

"I haven't gotten older, Max. I've gotten better."

"So I see."

Up the hall the front door opened and closed. A voice full of anxiety rumbled toward them.

"Please. Somebody help me with these bags of ice!"

Pat was back.

Carol-Anne. Max's new friend.

About five feet nine, a hundred and forty pounds. Full bosom, round hips. Older. Late late thirties, Samone surmised. There was a beauty to her, but it lay undiscovered beneath the short brown hair, a smidgen of lipstick, and eyebrows in need of plucking. She had on a simple white tee, inexpensive jeans, and no-name leather sneakers. No rings, no jewelry except for her Timex watch. Neither stylish nor a knockout,

Carol-Anne was the type of woman who never drew attention or turned a head.

Carol-Anne's skin was a pretty reddish brown, and her eyes did come alive when she smiled, but Samone saw nothing about the woman that would draw Max's heart.

Samone found herself staring. Tried to reason out how this plain Jane unsophisticated woman had come into Max's life. She couldn't see Carol-Anne escorting Max to his fancy company parties. Could not see her on the arm of Max anywhere. Did not understand how Max had fallen for a woman so different from herself.

Samone stared at Carol-Anne's daughter, Nadia, envious and jealous of the adoration Max displayed: fawning over Nadia, looking more like her daddy than her mother's "friend." These two people, coming into Max's life, fulfilling his world in a way Samone never got the chance to.

Old pain found her. It twisted her stomach in knots and took the ease from her eyes. She forced herself to stop looking, fighting off old sorrow of a man and a baby long gone. She shoved the pain to the bottom of her sandals and, with every step she took, crushed it to the ground.

Resentment passed as the party progressed. Old habits came into play. When Pat and Ray cut the cake and spooned out the ice cream, it was Samone and Max who served the guests. As Shamika opened presents, Pat snapped pictures and Ray shot the video, and Samone and Max retrieved loose wrapping paper and stacked the opened gifts. It was what they had done at Shamika's other birthday parties. It didn't make sense to change now. Only once had Samone caught Max's friend staring.

Only once.

17

Samone closed her appointment book and opened her saddle bag. Her fingers took inventory as she searched for her cigarettes and lighter: envelopes, rubber bands, loose tobacco, lipstick, a plastic comb. Her foundation powder, a small phone book, safety pens. Tampon holder, bits of paper, a pen, house keys, paper clips. A matchbook with no matches, a movie listing tossed in the bag so long ago that it was faded, soft and fuzzy like velvet. . . . *I really got to clean this bag out, I can't find shit in here.* Then finally, hiding as though they didn't want to be found, were her cigarettes; but she still hadn't found her lighter.

She checked her desk drawer and came up empty. Was about to go through her bag again when something said *Check your jacket pocket.* Sure enough, it was there.

Then, with everything at the ready, the cigarette in her mouth and a nice bluish white flame shooting up from her lighter, Samone was about to inhale when there was a light tap on her office door.

She looked at her wall clock and saw that it was five minutes to quitting time. Throughout her floor, desk drawers were opening and closing, file cabinets were being locked, and every available outside line was lit up with people making personal calls. People were ready to go home.

Laying aside her cigarette, Samone spoke loudly enough to get her voice to the other side of the door.

"Come in."

She must have been in a fight, was Samone's first thought, that or somebody had died. Merissa's hair was out of place, her cheeks puffy and flushed. Her eyes were wild and scary. They skittered about her office like brush fire.

"Merissa?"

"I've been a damn receptionist for over three years. Later for this shit. . . ." Her eyes lit up. "I want to file a grievance." With her hand on the knob and her feet still planted firmly on the burgundy hall carpet, Merissa seemed to have no intention of coming in.

"What happened?" Samone asked. That was what Merissa was waiting for: a sign of humanity, that Samone would care enough to listen to whatever she had to say.

Door closed, Merissa stood staring, her arms folded determinedly across her breast.

"I don't believe this shit. I've been passed up three

times already. Three fucking times I apply for a position and they tell me no. I've been a fucking receptionist for three years and they still won't take me. . . . Can I sit down?''

"Sure."

''It ain't fair, Samone . . . they're not going to get away with this shit, that's all I know.''

''Who, Merissa? Who?''

The long red nails flew around her, indicating the walls of Samone's office. ''Them . . . Harris, Dorothy, Andrea. All of them.''

Samone saw each face as Merissa read the roll call. They were all personnel managers. For a moment she wondered why she had escaped the list. The answer came swiftly. Because Samone was black.

''You applied for Mark's vacancy?''

Merissa's eyes were hot upon her. In a blink of an eye, Samone became part of that other camp. In a blink of an eye, Samone had become a ''them.''

''You know I did.''

Samone nodded, carefully watching Merissa's fever. ''I'm sorry, you're right. I remember now.'' But she had forgotten. Passing Merissa over for positions was so common that Samone had stopped counting the times she and the other personnel managers had sat around the conference room, looked at their receptionist's application, and given it the thumbsdown.

Besides that, prior to this moment, the bitch never gave Samone any indication that she even liked her.

Samone eyed the clock: three minutes to quitting time. She reached for her cigarette.

"I was about to have one, you don't mind."

"No, go ahead. It's your office."

Samone inhaled, letting go a rush of blue gray smoke. Leaned forward.

"They want college degrees," was how Samone began. "They want a BA from anywhere in anything, as long as it's a BA."

"That's just an excuse, Samone. Did Andrea have one?"

"No, but Andrea got the job right before they changed the requirements."

"Or did they change it when I started applying?"

"Come on, Merissa. It's not personal."

"Isn't it, though? I've applied for every other clerical position in this place, and haven't gotten one. Now what does that sound like to you? You of all people should know."

"If you're talking discrimination . . ." *And that's exactly what's she talking, Samone. You know it like she does.*

"My mother always said, If the kettle's black . . ."

"Yeah, but Merissa, that's a serious charge."

"Will you get off it, Samone? Just once, get off that shit. How long you been here? How many black or Hispanic personnel managers have they had at any given time? One. And that one is you. You think that's a fucking accident?"

"That's not the point."

"Oh, yeah. I'd expect that coming from you. After

all, you their number one player . . . you play their game so well, you living their life.''

Is she talking about me and Jon? Calling me an Oreo . . . what does this bitch know about anything, especially me?

"Look, Merissa, *you* came here, remember? I didn't ask you in.''

"Was a waste of my time. I should have known.''

"Look, you wanna play it your way, then you go right ahead. Write your grievance. And you know where that's going to get you? Fired . . . don't you understand? They care two shits about you. So you go ahead, you give them a reason to get rid of you. 'Cause Lord knows somebody's got a sister or a cousin ready to take your place.'' Samone saw the pain in Merissa's eyes. Knew her words had been unkind, but they were full of truth, and regardless, Merissa had to be warned.

"So what are you saying?'' This was a new Merissa, one full of fear and confusion. Samone felt sorry for her, because anger in the workplace got you shit, and that's all Merissa had now—anger.

Samone put out her cigarette and opened her desk drawer. It was five o'clock. Time to go.

"I'm saying, me and you are going to get out of here. Number one, this isn't the place to talk, and number two, it's five o'clock. Okay?''

They didn't talk much as they headed to McCann's, which was just fine with the both of them. Like a balloon suddenly untied, the anger and apprehension had released itself and left them, once again with no common ground.

This wasn't the greatest of ideas. I don't even know why I opened my mouth and volunteered my services like this. It ain't like I don't have a place to go, like home. A place I'd rather be than walking fast track next to my receptionist, who for the last three years never had two words for me, but suddenly finds herself in need of my services. . . .

The air was tight with tension as they waited for the light to change. And when the light turned green, Merissa didn't move. Samone, certain that she had, was in the middle of the street before she realized Merissa was still at the curb.

There was a quiet desperation about Merissa as she stood there, trying hard to do this solo, forgoing the assistance she had wanted not ten minutes before.

"Go ahead, Samone. I'll be all right."

This child really ought to get over it. It's not the end of the world.

But she don't know that, Samone. She ain't you. . . .

It was in that moment that Samone realized just how wrong she had been about Merissa; her show of being a "get mine" wench wasn't who she was at all. Merissa was nothing but a little girl trying damn hard to show the world different. Something we've all been guilty of, Samone realized as she backtracked across the street, reaching out her hand.

"Come on, girlfriend. You got me out here, now let's go somewhere and talk this thing over."

"You got other things to do."

"That's true . . . I got laundry and dishes and even my nails, but if the Great and Terrible Merissa comes to my office for my help, then you know it's important."

Merissa's voice slipped into the one she preferred, New Yorican. "Yeah, ain't that something," she said, eyeing Samone as suspicion moved into trust.

Samone smiled and patted her back. "We'll figure something out."

With this new awkward bond holding them loosely together, they headed toward the bar.

"I always wanted to be a producer."

Samone nodded, her drink nearly gone, taking with it the rough edges. Her mood, laid-back, was the perfect audience to Merissa's monologue.

"That was my plan, you know. Get in the door and then get a production assistant's position."

Samone nodded again, her fingers reaching for her burning cigarette, bringing it slowly to her lips. Somewhere behind her—or was it to her left?—jazz was being played. For a second she tried to catch a complete rift, but it was lost in the buzz of conversation, in the tinkle of glasses and the rush of laughter. A jangle of fuzzy busyness was constantly arriving from all directions.

Across from her Merissa talked on, excited and hyped by Samone's promise to speak to Harris on her behalf. Merissa wasn't one of his favorite people, so it probably wouldn't make a difference. But who knew? Maybe the threat of a grievance would. Maybe it wouldn't. . . .

Samone glanced at her watch. It was getting late. Besides that, she was hungry and just a tiny bit drunk. She stopped Merissa midsentence.

"I hate to cut this short, but I have to get out of here."

"Yeah. Sure . . . thanks."

"Don't go thanking me yet. I still have to talk to Harris."

"No, not just that. I mean talking to me. And being straight about it."

"Ain't no thing, Merissa. Ain't no big deal."

But Merissa knew that Samone was lying. It was a very big deal.

For nine years Samone had been in the background, playing by their rules, never making waves. Understood and accepted that she was just a *token,* and not of appreciation. No fool, with eyes wide open, Samone had settled back and accepted the stance. Become a good ol' girl in the good ol' boys' network. Never giving much, never caring.

Walk that walk, talk that talk. *Yas, Sur, Massa Harris, Sur.* Being the Good Negro; living the Plantation Life, nineties style.

They had never taken her seriously. Samone had never demanded it of herself and therefore never demanded it of them—Harris, Dorothy, and Claire. Until yesterday, she had been a *them.* But that was no longer possible. Merissa had changed that.

Samone realized that she was the one people of color looked to when they applied for a position. She *was* their hope. There was no one else.

Samone had a responsibility. To Merissa and to herself.

The next morning, bright and early, she went down the hall to Harris's office.

Harris *was* the personnel department.

Independent thought was not allowed. No one crossed him, no one dared utter an opinion too far from his own. The last person Harris expected to hear a personal plea on Merissa's behalf from was Samone. Harris had never known her to care for any applicant, one way or the other.

He didn't interrupt, waiting for her to finish; annoyed and leery of this new Samone who cared— about Merissa, no less. When she finished, Harris shrugged.

"College degree."

He expected her gone about then. Expected Samone to turn on her heels and leave, embarrassed by her new show of concern; apprehensive that she'd even attempted to change his mind. Harris would always remember this moment—Samone's show of independence. She had to know he'd hold it against her.

Harris had already mentally dismissed her when he realized she was still there; there and speaking. Her voice came at him like tiny pointy daggers, slicing through his defense like paper.

"Well then, I'll suggest to Merissa that she enroll

in night classes and work on her degree. She wants to get into production. A BA in media studies is what she needs. NBS will pay her tuition because it's job related. So what if it costs the company more in time and money than if we just give her a production assistant spot? Hey, rules are rules.''

Harris studied her. Saw the cool smile. Arms relaxed at her sides. Her eyes unhard, normal. Eased; they could have just shared a good joke. Samone, relaxed in the aftermath, was no longer afraid. It was over. Done. Her first stand.

Hardball, Samone was playing hardball. Harris was shocked that she'd even figured it out and had prepared herself well enough to do battle with him

Worse, she was absolutely right. They would have to put Merissa through school. She would get her BA, and there would be few barriers left.

Harris did not want Merissa anywhere but at his receptionist desk. She was a part of his Affirmative Action stance. Merissa hated him but feared him. It was easy keeping her in line. Who knew who they'd get to replace her.

Samone stood there, her smile as cool as a cucumber. *The lesser of two evils, Harris. You decide.*

Harris played with the knot in his tie.

Samone had him by the balls. And it hurt, bad. Not as dumb as she looked, not by any means. He knew he had two choices, and he wanted neither of them. It was all Samone's fault. He would never forget that.

He picked through a stack of papers, pulling out the job description for production assistant. He would not look at her. Spoke to the paper instead. "*Espiritos.* Be right up her alley, won't it."

"I think she'd like it," Samone said.

Harris glared at her, his anger rising. "She? Since when did you care about Merissa?" He saw a flicker in her eyes. A nerve had been touched. He felt better already. He gave Samone a scrutinizing look, determined not to let her walk away unscathed. "I've never known you to care about anything much, Samone."

But Samone was not fazed. Was no longer afraid. She looked down at her department manager, with the three-thousand-dollar hair replacement and the home in Cos Cob, Connecticut, and said nothing. Yes, she was guilty, but she didn't have to admit it to him.

Samone brightened her smile, her lips parting to reveal shiny, opaque teeth. He waited for her to respond, but all she would give was her smile. There was no need for words; what she had just accomplished said it all.

Cautiously, carefully, Samone turned. Opened the door and walked out. A feather moving on a breeze, she coasted down the hall. Closed office doors with brass nameplates, "Claire Rikes," "Dorothy Sheen," slipping from view.

The last office, "Samone L. Lewis." Black lettering on shiny brass. For the first time ever, that name meant something, was important.

With careful fingers Samone twisted the doorknob. A blast of cool air rushed her. She leaned against the closed door and shut her eyes. Her legs betrayed her calm, shaking from a rush of adrenaline. Samone took deep breaths. Opened her eyes. Looked around and knew she had survived.

Later, she called Merissa into her office.

"How does *Espiritos* sound to you?"

"Are you kidding me?"

"Monday morning. Be on the set at seven A.M."

"Oh . . . thank you. Thank you so much, Samone."

"Now, look. You got this far, so no screwing up, all right? Somebody get on your last nerve, and you know they will, just walk away. Take five . . . don't let nobody take from you what you've rightfully gotten, understand?

"It ain't an easy job or a pretty one. You're going to be a glorified 'gofer,' you're gonna be going for this, and going for that. You are at the bottom of a very long and very powerful totem pole. Production assistants have gotten fired 'cause a guest didn't like the way they looked . . . so enjoy the rest of this week . . . and hey, after work, go celebrate."

There was a soft ease in the room now. The type of camaraderie neither had been afforded in a long time. It was funny how things worked out. Just when they were getting friendly, Merissa was moving on.

"I have to take you to dinner," Merissa decided last minute.

"You don't have to." But already Samone was looking forward to it.

"Of course I do. You like Spanish food?"

"Most of the time."

"Good. There's this great little restaurant. You'll love it. . . . Tell me, did Jon ever tell you about how he got your number?"

"He said something about raiding the files. Why?"

Merissa smiled, flipping her red nails in Samone's direction. "It was me . . . I gave it to him."

Summer was at its finest, warm and breezy, as Samone and Jon window-shopped Third Avenue on their way to Lord & Taylor's.

They weren't buying a damn thing, but the proprietors and sales clerks didn't know that. All they knew was what they saw: an attractive interracial couple in love, paying close attention to whatever caught their eye.

Samone tried on three-hundred-dollar shoes, and Jon hoisted up framed reprints as though he were trying to imagine them on his living room wall.

One-skinned, they moved through the stores. Sales managers shooed away clerks, offering charm, concern, and free delivery.

And while Samone and Jon played the game of "yes, I have to have this" convincingly, and at one point got real crazy over a ten-thousand-dollar original watercolor, the only place they would be spending his money today was Lord & Taylor's.

On the streets, Samone was consumed with the spirit of the day and the newfound power in loving Jon. He hadn't taken a damn thing from her, but he'd made her stronger. Only a strong love could survive a world that still said they had no right being together.

But nobody had the right to question her love for him. Not her momma. Not even her daddy. A fierce love full of fire was moving through her, and nothing was going to take that away. Because beyond white skin and hair fine as silk; beyond custom, tradition, and racism; Jon was there for her.

She didn't have to mold herself to suit him; he accepted her for all that she was and wasn't. Jon loved her completely, and that was something no man had done in a long time.

Lord & Taylor's. Samone's fantasy made flesh.

"What do you think?" she asked, stepping out of the dressing room.

Jon touched the material of the short red dress, his fingers uncareful as they moved over the curve of her hip and flirted with the rise of her behind, where they lingered before she swatted them away.

"I like it."

"You don't think it's a little too tight? I mean, I can hardly breathe in this thing."

"You look sensational."

"You see the price tag, maybe you won't think so."

"What fun is having a credit card if you can't splurge?"

"Well, in that case, I'm definitely going to have to get some new pumps and a bag. You can't wear a four-hundred-dollar dress with old stuff."

"How did I know that?"

"You didn't. Be back."

She'd need a tennis outfit, a pair of tennis shoes, and a racket. Maybe she'd get a new bathing suit for the hell of it.

Jon was taking her to Montauk.

The next weekend, Samone took him to New Jersey.

Images of Samone were everywhere.

At the age of four on the beach; chubby legs rising to meet the swimsuit hitched high on her thigh. The plastic sunglasses with Mickey Mouse ears shielding her intent; her tiny body leaning to the left, impatient with the camera and eager for the ocean all in one moment.

At five, in her red wool coat, looking uncooperative on the lap of a white-faced Santa. At seven, staring bright eyed and oh so smiley in her white blouse and red Scotch plaid hair ribbons. On ice skates in Central Park at the age of nine.

Hovering over her eleventh birthday cake with more lit candles than she'd ever be.

Fourteen years old, sporting a huge afro, various red, black, and green buttons adorning her blue denim jacket. The afro resulting in much conflict in the Lewis household when Samone refused to go back to the beauty parlor and the straightening comb. Samone thinking her parents horrible, phony, and ''nothing but a bunch of Oreos.''

Jessica tried to explain that the afro was a throwback to Tarzan movies and blackface. Tried to explain that not only was it unsightly, it was uncomely and certainly unhealthy. . . . *Samone, anything fall down in all the hair, it would take weeks to find.*

Jessica tried to explain that it made Samone look wild, untamed. That the police harassed the Black Panthers and a cop could assume she was one of them and shoot to kill. That Samone was just asking for trouble, especially with those asinine buttons that shouted "KILL THE PIGS!" and "POWER TO THE PEOPLE"; and *What decent young man would want a young lady with wild nappy hair and crazy sayings pinned all over her like some freak in a sideshow!*

Samone had been so into the Black Power thing, as if she had been empty all her life up until that moment and the movement had found her and filled her.

Baptized African Methodist Episcopalian, a Sunday school monitor with blue-and-white satin ribbons that said so, Samone had stopped going to church. She'd denounced it as dogmatic rhetoric.

Jessica just knew her daughter was losing her mind, what with Samone sneaking off to rallies up on 125th Street and putting up posters of Bobby Seale and Huey Newton as if they had become her God. Listening to The Last Poets and Gil Scott-Heron over and over again. Playing her tinny-sounding portable stereo *loud . . .* for hours, "On the subway, I dug a mannn digging meeee . . ." and "The revolution will not be televised" escaping through the closed door of Samone's bedroom.

It had been a frightening time, dispelling all that Jessica and Odell had tried to instill in Samone. And while Jessica knew and respected that changes were needed, carrying guns and inciting the police wasn't the way to do it. The call to arm yourself and take to the streets was a frightening and dangerous means of challenging those in power. Martin Luther King Jr. had the right idea, not gun-toting, beret-wearing black men stirring up the people into a frenzy—her daughter included. This was what Jessica had concluded at the time.

But now here, decades coming and going. With information of government sabotage and assassination, Jessica decided maybe the Black Panthers had been more in tune with the times than they'd been given credit.

Here among the pictures of her daughter's life, maybe Jessica had been wrong. Maybe being black and proud and militant was the way to be. That maybe in trying to deny Samone her need to verify and empower her blackness, Jessica had succeeded. This was her last thought as Odell called to her to "come and get dressed. They'll be here soon."

Bearing what? Jessica thought quietly, wishing for a cigarette and to put away the pictures in the same instant. But even as she pushed the shoebox back onto the hall closet shelf, the image of her daughter at fourteen, standing black, proud, and determined, lingered like the smoke from her cigarette. In no rush to go away.

You are your mother's daughter, Jessica found herself thinking as she eyed Jon for the second time in her life, up close and personal.

He's handsome. But what boy Samone ever brought home wasn't? A nice smile, brown hair. Strange cat eyes. Jessica smiled, extending her hand, hoping her polish had dried.

He's seeing the Samone in me. He's noticing how much we're alike. . . . I shouldn't stare, but when was the last time a young white man was courting my daughter?

"This is my father, Odell Lewis," Samone was saying.

I feel the smirk on my face, watching my husband lift his hand to the boy's. I feel Odell's thoughts: he's thinking, What an ignorant white boy. Ignorant and arrogant in thinking Odell will be a gracious receiver. That Odell will ease this uncomfortable moment . . . which he won't. He never had much use for white people.

Jon accepted the firm handshake. Did not wince as Samone's father's hand squeezed his own like a vise.

Young man, you have a whole lot of proving to do, Jessica decided, her smile a smug and certain thing. *Odell is seconds from declaring war on your hide.*

She indulged herself a laugh and hugged her daughter. Life was strange. Just when you think you had it down pat, there's always a twist in the road.

"Daddy?"

"Up here."

Samone climbed the carpeted stairs, feeling the

strangeness she always felt when she visited. She had never lived in the house.

Long after Samone had moved into her own place, Jessica and Odell had journeyed from the enclave of Sugar Hill in Harlem to a quiet cul-de-sac in Teaneck, New Jersey.

As she made her way, the late afternoon sun painted tangerine pictures on the wood-paneled walls. It was a quiet and peaceful excursion, but Samone felt like an intruder nonetheless.

The guest room door was ajar, meaning her father was no doubt inside, reading his paper or indulging himself his pipe. How she missed the smell of cherrywood tobacco stinking up the two-bedroom brownstone. Her mother raising windows and fussing all in the same breath. *So long ago, Daddy. Long time ago. But here I am and there you are. Just inside the door of the room that in another lifetime would have been mine.*

"Hi," Samone said, pensive on the threshold.

Her father's pipe waved her in.

"Just taking a smoke," Odell offered, taking a pull.

"Mommy still won't let you smoke nowhere but here?"

"This time of year, I normally go out on the deck."

Samone paused. There were words to be said, and nothing in her wanted to begin. Jon was downstairs with her mother, keeping her company as she fussed around the kitchen, making last minute preparations for dinner soon to be served.

"He's not as bad as you think, now, is he?"

"He look fine. He talk fine. He's mannerly and attentive. But he's still white."

"Which is it that you don't like—him or the color of his skin?"

"You know the answer."

"Daddy, don't you think I can determine what's best for me?"

A thick cloud moved slowly over the sun; the room rushed into dimness. Samone squinted in the gloom, her father momentarily obliterated by darkness and pale blue smoke.

"So you've told me."

"Be fair about it, that's all. Yes, I know you don't know him from Adam. And all you know is that he's not the same color as you and me. But there's a whole lot more to him. He treats me good, Daddy. Real good. He's my friend as well. And I really really care for him."

The pipe was poised before her father's brown lips. It waited for the answer, already known, to be spoken.

"You love him?"

"You know I do."

"Then what I think or feel won't matter."

"It'll always matter."

"Samone, you bring him here to my house, because you felt we should meet. Your mother gets me up early yesterday to help her clean and take her food shopping. This morning she got me running around doing this and doing that. . . . Nobody asked me what I wanted."

It was an old wound talking, started over thirty-seven years ago when her mother had accepted her father's proposal. It was the way of the Chisolm women. The men went out and worked, and the women ran the household. Mostly it was a smooth arrangement. But every now and then it caused her father grief. Odell had stopped arguing about it years ago.

"I'm sorry, Daddy."

"Yeah, I know, baby."

Samone moved into the room. The cloud passed. Sunlight spilled into the window, bathing her father in precious light. He tapped his pipe against the large amber glass ashtray and laid it aside.

Odell stood, stretched. Walked toward her.

He stopped in front of her, his hands light about her shoulders, his eyes intense and focused.

"You really love him?"

Samone had never been so afraid. "Yes, I do."

"He loves you?"

"For a long time."

"Of course he would. You're a prize and he knows it. He respects you?"

"Yes, he does."

"You respect him?"

"As much as a Chisolm woman can."

Her father smiled. It was an answer he had known all too personally. After all, Samone was her mother's child.

"Don't let any man walk over you. No matter what color he is."

Samone laughed, a needed ease moving through

her. Her father wasn't at the point where she had wanted him to be with the business between her and Jon, but he was closer.

"Samone! Odell! Come on downstairs now. You two been up there long enough."

Her father placed his arm around her shoulder, moving her toward the stairs. "I swear, Samone, nobody can call the hogs like your momma can."

"She swears she was always a city girl, but Aunt Kate says she used to spend summers on the farm down in Georgia."

At the bottom of the stairs, Jessica waited. Her oatmeal dress and milky pearls contrasted with her white cooking apron. Impatience was the hand on her hip and her face set stern.

"Come on, you two."

"We're coming, Jess, hold your horses."

It was a comfortable conspiracy Samone felt as she and her father made their way down the steps, arms tight about each other, her father's wide girth making the passage careful and full of gentle caution.

The living room was full of light as the sun began to deepen into the horizon. Going down in a blaze of red, it tinted all things sienna.

"Dinner will be ready in a minute. Jon, you ever have candied yams and collards?"

"No. But I love sweet-potato pie and have had kale."

Odell sat up. "Kale? What do you know about kale?"

Jon turned slightly, addressing Samone's father. "Well, let's see. You separate the leaves and wash them. Throw away the stems. Boil up some smoked meat and put the leaves on top. Simmer to tender, if I remember."

"Where you from?" Odell asked, a new respect creeping into his voice.

Jon caught Samone watching this exchange between the two men who loved her. He smiled, his answer ready and full of wit.

"Malibu."

Odell laughed, and Jessica clucked her teeth.

In the end, Odell decided that if it had to be a white boy, it might as well be Jon. Whereas Jessica, polite and obliging, held off final thoughts. Nobody knew her daughter the way she did. Jon may have been the flavor of the month, but time would be the ultimate test.

Still, Jessica wished her daughter well.

"Will you please hold it down? I can't hear the game." Ray grabbed the remote control, pointed the device toward the television, and raised the volume. From the kitchen, the smell of baked chicken, macaroni and cheese, and collard greens filtered in the air. Ray had planned to get his plate during half-time. Doze toward the last quarter if the Knicks managed to get a good lead. A nice quiet Sunday, or so he thought.

But then Samone had appeared at his front door, her eyes giddy with news. It was then that Ray knew his quiet afternoon was shot to pieces. Samone was there to tell her business and be loud with his wife. And for the past five minutes that was all they had been doing.

"Now, Ray, as long as you've known me, have you ever known me to be quiet?"

"I keep hoping old age will catch up with you."

"Samone," Pat piped, so very glad to be keeping company with her best friend, "don't pay him no mind. He's just mad 'cause his team's losing."

Ray turned, casting his wife an evil look. Pat blew him a kiss. Said, "Love you," meaning it. Still in love with his skin the color of new pennies and the freckles across his nose.

In that moment, Pat realized she still loved the light brown of his eyes and even the beginnings of his receding hairline. That after all these years, she still loved her husband very much.

"Come on, Pat, let's go in another room."

Pat pointed up the hall. "Bedroom. The air conditioner's on."

Samone lay across the bed, and Pat took up camp near the headboard.

"Now, tell me again. Jon said what when your father asked him about kale?"

"Said he was from Malibu. Pat, I'd like to fall out on the floor. It was so funny and so *white,* you know? But perfect. You should have seen Odell's face when he realized Jon was making fun."

"Too much. So it turned out nice, then?"

"Better than I expected. I just knew my father

would be waiting at the front door with his hunting rifle.''

"And you say your mom called you later, talking about how she thought Jon was nice?"

"Pat, she sure 'nough did. I tell you, I'm still in shock."

"Well, I guess I'm next."

"You're gonna behave?"

"Don't I always?"

"No."

"I promise. I'll be good. I'll make him dinner—dry-ass tuna on white, with a Diet Coke on the side."

Samone smirked. "Funny, Pat. Real funny."

Pat thought about it minute.

"I think I like him already."

Samone removed the pan of lasagna from the oven and sat it on the stove. She eyed the clock and saw that she had exactly twenty minutes to shower and get dressed. Since morning she had been busier than a bee in a hive, cleaning, mopping, sweeping, and shining. She had cleaned her apartment as though it were New Year's Eve.

Guess who's coming to dinner . . . Pat, Ray, and Jon.

Jon put the white wine on the living room table, his eyes eager on everything.

"Not here yet?" he asked, cautious.

"They called about two minutes before you got here. Running late, but on their way."

He smiled at her. "Nervous?"

Samone gave him a close-lipped smile. "No, not much. . . . You?"

Jon shrugged. "She's your best friend, right?"

"Can't be no worse than meeting my parents."

"I don't know about that. Anything I can do?"

"Can you cut up the Italian bread? I'll be right back."

Jon went to the kitchen, Samone to the bathroom.

The knife, in dire need of sharpening, resisted the crust. Jon was searching the kitchen drawer for something to sharpen it with when the intercom buzzed. Without thought, he went to answer.

A few minutes later, when the doorbell rang, Samone cracked open the bathroom door and asked Jon to get it.

"Hi. I'm the white guy," was how he introduced himself. "You're in the right place. Samone's in the bathroom. Come on in."

Pat extended her hand, her eyes never far from Jon's face. So this was Mr. Jon. Mr. White Man. The white man bad enough to steal her best friend's heart. Wasn't hard to see why. All you had to do was look at them eyes and that skin more olive than white, smiling like he was about to shit his pants, Pat thought.

"I'm Pat," she offered, willing to ease up the moment.

"Of course, who else could you be?"

Ray stepped in, extending his hand. "Raymond Chadaway."

They shook hands, both embarrassed about being there. After all, this had everything to do with Samone and Pat and not a whole lot to do with them. It was about Pat accepting or rejecting the new man in Samone's life.

"Nice to meet you. Go ahead in. Samone'll be out in a minute." Jon went back to kitchen duty.

A minute later he heard a squeal go up in the living room. Heard Pat mumble something and Samone's laughter seeking him out. Knew that some major milestone had been reached.

"I told you, Pat," Samone said, loud enough for Jon to hear.

"I know, I know," Jon was saying as they sat around the kitchen table, "you were expecting blond hair and blue eyes, and me talking like 'hey, dude,' and 'totally,' right?"

Pat smiled unwillingly. "Well, white and from California, that's what I would have expected."

"See, that's what's wrong with America," Jon began.

Samone put her hands up. "There will be no talking about America, stereotypes, or racism. We are here to enjoy my food and have a nice time, okay?"

"The lasagna is good, Samone. When you learn to cook?" was what Ray wanted to know.

"Ray, don't even try it. You know I can cook."

"The last time I was here, you couldn't."

"Well, you ain't been here in a while."

Ray nodded. "Gotten better. Maybe I'll come back again."

"Why, thank you, Raymond. Now, you all save room for my dessert."

"What's for dessert?" Pat wanted to know.

"Oh, Lord, Samone done baked something again. Hey, Jon, Samone ever make you a cake?" Ray asked, spearing a slice of cucumber from his plate.

"No, why?"

"Take my word for it, man, you don't want her to."

"Hey, that's not fair." She looked at Jon. "It was the first time I ever baked a homemade cake . . . got a little burnt."

Pat corrected her. "A little, Samone? Thing was so black on the outside, I thought it was chocolate."

"And hard, too. Could have hammered some nails with it," Ray added.

"Well, I'll have you all know that I didn't make dessert this time. I bought it. Cheesecake."

Pat smiled. "What kind?"

"What else? Lindy's, of course."

"What's a Lindy's?" Jon asked, lightening the mood.

18

Labor Day. The official end of summer. Samone closed her eyes. Sighed.

No matter how bright the sun shone or how hot the day, there was always something maudlin and bitter-sweet about Labor Day. Maybe it was a leftover from her school days, where this holiday always meant the long vacation was over and it was back to school. Back to structured days, homework, and studying.

Whatever the reason, Labor Day always put a funny kind of ache in Samone's heart, as if the best of times were over. She could feel an eagerness for the transition of fall, the time of year when her heart started seeking a warm place to spend the winter. This year she didn't have to look far.

Still, as she got up and took a shower, taking an extra five minutes in the mirror to pluck her eyebrows, her mind evoked other Labor Days. Other places, other faces. She would never stop hearing the love in Max's mother's voice as she called for Samone to "come help out in the kitchen" or "go ask Mr. Scutter what did he do with the ice pick."

Mostly it was "This is Max's girlfriend, Samone. Ain't she something? They are gonna make me some beautiful grandchildren." Max's mother hoped Samone and Max would get married and have lots of children. Even as Samone told herself that that was her old life, that there would be no more Mrs. Scutters, the memories refused to go away.

No indeed. There's not gonna be a Mrs. Everette, calling me to her kitchen and parading me around in front of all her family and friends. Jon will never help his father serve drinks or tend the grill. There are no Mrs. Scutters in Jon's world. There's just me.

Samone stared at herself in the mirror. She told herself she was checking to make sure the arches in her brows were neat. But there were worse lies she had told. Samone was searching her soul to see if her last thought had sunk in. As she looked into the cocoa powder irises, she knew that it had.

19

Samone looked at her watch. Around her sat Andrea, Dorothy, and Harris. In front of them were seven in-house résumés for an associate producer's position for *Espiritos*.

Samone rubbed her eyes. It was an hour past lunch and she was hungry, weary, and agitated.

She looked at no one, her hand reaching for a cigarette, ignoring the No Smoking sign on the wall. She half listened to the voices around her in the time it took to light it.

When she couldn't take any more, Samone spoke up. Enough of the bullshit.

"Excuse me," she began, her voice as sharp, clear, and resounding as a high school principal quieting an assembly. "We seem to be getting nowhere fast. Why don't we break for lunch and come back."

Andrea looked up from her empty coffee cup. "Harris?"

He studied Samone for a long time. Irritated but resigned, he agreed.

"Be back no later than two. I have a three o'clock."

Samone gathered up the ashtray, her empty cup, cigarettes, and lighter. Pushed in her chair and moved to the door, her mind heavy with consequences.

It's Merissa's spot, plain and simple. Her first three months she was on time, courteous, and Vincent had nothing but praise for her. Four of her story ideas went into production, and she's joined the guild. What more do they need? Why are they pussyfooting?

If they're not going to consider her because nobody likes her, then damn it, they should just say it. Stand up and say, "We are not considering her because she was such a bitch with us, she doesn't deserve it." But don't insult me. Don't sit around wasting my time.

Samone went to the corner, got two hot dogs and a can of C&C grape soda. Went back to her office and ate without pleasure, her eye never far from the clock.

She's not going to get it. They're not going to let her. She got out of the clerical pool, and that's as far as they're gonna let her go. Associate producer? We're talking about fifteen thousand dollars more a year and three steps away from being a producer. No way are they gonna let her have that kind of power.

Unless I can convince them. But can I? Can I convince the sheep not to follow the shepherd?

Samone looked at the clock. It was twenty minutes to two.

She burped, painful and offensive. As she fanned the air before her, her mind moved, seeking solutions. Her phone rang.

"Samone Lewis," she answered crisply.

"I need to see you in my office." Harris hung up before she could tell him yes, no, or otherwise.

"Have a seat."

Samone took one, determined not to show her fear.

He leaned back, swiveled in his black leather executive chair. Studied her, none too pleased with his findings.

He leaned forward. "Your annual review is coming up." His eyebrow raised. "Scratching backs, Samone. That's what this business is really about."

She felt the rise in her voice and could not contain it. "I do my job well, Harris."

"Ah, but those latenesses . . ."

Samone looked away.

"For years I've ignored them. Said to myself, Samone's a team player, so what if she doesn't get here by nine?" He addressed the air above her head. "Then one day Samone decides not to play ball." He paused, looked at her. "No ball, no privileges."

"Is that a threat?" Samone wanted to know.

Harris pretended to be stunned, but he was known for his drama. "Threat? Not at all . . . *fact.*" The word pierced her soul. "Fact is you're always late." He picked up a piece of paper off his desk and handed it

to her. In heavy bold capital letters were the words
"WARNING NOTICE." Samone didn't have to read
any further to know that it was for her.

Harris took back the paper. "As you can see, it's
handwritten." More pausing, his gaze steady. "Your
vote determines whether or not Darlene gets to type
the official one."

Samone studied him. "You hate her that much,
Harris?"

"Who?"

"Merissa."

"I liked her fine."

"As a receptionist," Samone added, indignant.

Harris ignored her and stood up. Looked at his
watch. Acted as if he had just remembered something
he had to do, Samone forced to be audience to another
of his grand performances. "Look at the time. Got to
go." He smiled her way. "Thanks for coming by."
And walked out.

Samone sat there, numb. Realized where she was
and stood. The motion cleared her head.

In the time that Merissa had been transferred, Harris had treated Samone no differently. If anything, he
had given her freedom to voice her strong growing
opinions. He seemed to enjoy this new passionate Samone, which only fueled her fervor. Sometimes her
opinions were accepted and sometimes they were not,
but that was okay because that was the way it was
supposed to be.

Not once had Samone thought that Harris was waiting her out. That he was waiting for something she

really wanted to flex *his* muscle. But that's just what he had done.

Warning notice. Three offenses were all it took, and she was history. Her nine years at NBS down the drain. Just as she was beginning to feel a purpose in what she was doing, the rug had been pulled from under her.

Get to work on time.

Samone couldn't remember the last time she had. Her alarm was set fifteen minutes later than what it was supposed to be. She never prepared her clothes the night before. She took the local train because the express never had any seats.

She always stopped for breakfast, no matter how much after nine she arrived at work. Her whole regimen was based on her being late. Voting for Merissa would change that.

But could she get to work on time? Every day for the rest of her life? Even if she did nominate Merissa, nobody else would. So what was the point of risking a warning?

This is about more than Merissa. This is about me as much as it is about her.

Fail or succeed, Samone couldn't turn back now.

No one saw Samone standing in the door, cigarettes and lighter in one hand, a pen and her can of soda in the other.

"He's not going to place her," Andrea was saying.

Dorothy, bored with the whole thing, agreed.

''You're right. Harris can't stand her. And I never had much use for her, either.''

''I really don't care who gets it at this point,'' Andrea decided.

Dorothy closed her eyes and reached for a résumé. ''Let's take this one.''

Andrea laughed. ''Sure, just reach in blind and pick one. Good, Dorothy, real good.''

Dorothy moved her fingers through the résumés again. ''Okay, okay, this one.''

Andrea grabbed it and looked it over. ''This one? He's still on probation. Hasn't been here long enough to get health insurance.'' She eased back into her chair, nudging the left heel out of her shoe. ''Hell, I really don't care.''

''Well, you should,'' Samone said, coming into both their lines of vision.

''Oh, Samone. I didn't see you.''

''Look,'' she began, closing the door, ''we all know Merissa is the one for the job. And we can get her the position.''

''Harris hates her,'' Dorothy offered matter-of-factly.

''Oh, so you have to, too?''

Andrea's voice was full of insinuation.

''Come on, Samone. You know how she treated us, you included.''

Me included? And why the fuck wouldn't I be included? I'm a manager just like you. . . .

''Regardless,'' Samone said, moving forward. The need to get Merissa what she rightfully deserved intense, "Vincent wants her. You're going need a real reason, and it can't be because you don't like her."

Dorothy studied Samone: hair carefully done and wearing an Evan Picone suit today. Samone had been dressing first-class lately. More gifts from the rich white boyfriend on the ninth floor, she supposed.

"Harris *is* the director of personnel, you know."

"So what are we, chopped liver? Is that why we spent two hours this morning and are about to do another hour because what we think doesn't count?" Samone pulled out a chair, leaned on the back. "Look, for years we've been kissing Harris's butt, for what? Is that why we're here? We are just as important as he is. We have the right to independent thought and decisions. Aren't you tired of being afraid of offending Harris? I know I am."

Dorothy looked away. Andrea gathered the scattered résumés into a single pile.

"Even if you don't care, you should at least vote for what's right. Not for what Harris wants, but for what is fair," was Samone's final word before she sat down.

A minute later Harris entered. He scooped up the résumés and checked his watch. Looked around the room at all of them. And then, one by one, he asked for their recommendations. Andrea nominated Gloria Phillips; Dorothy and Harris followed her lead.

Samone was the last to be asked.

"Merissa Gabòn." She said the name as though it were the first breath, the most precious two words in the world. She said it giving every syllable its due.

Gabòn. It rolled off her tongue like a waterfall. She wanted to make certain the name would haunt them in their dreams.

They stared at her. Three pairs of eyes, outraged and full of contempt. The very air fused with "How dare you?"

Samone took their disrespect with a huge grain of salt. Looked at each of them personally and privately and smiled, glad to have it over with. Understood that they resented her for things they knew nothing about. That they feared all that she was and all that she would become.

She stood without being given permission, gathered her wares about her, and walked out of the room. The need to cry nudged her toward the ladies' room. But she would not shed her tears. Not here. Not ever.

She was not there to hear the conversation that went on after her exit. Did not have to be there to know the words spoken, the accusations made.

From this point on she would be considered an outsider, a rebel. Hard, trying days lay ahead for her. But Samone would continue her struggle. She had done the right thing, and no one could take away the power of being right.

Samone lay across the bed the moment she got home. Outside, the world was cold and dark, but inside it was toasty and warm.

Thank God for something.

No bag of tricks this day had she pulled. She had promised herself that she wouldn't call. That she would just wait until Vincent introduced the new associate producer and let Merissa find out that way.

But Merissa deserved better.

Samone sat up and picked up the phone. She dialed the number and listened to it ring.

"Hola." Merissa's accent, fluent and full of music, was a pretty sound, Samone realized.

"Hey, Merissa, it's Samone."

"Samone, hi. *Qué pasa?*"

"Gloria Phillips."

"From the six o'clock news?"

"Yeah, her."

"Well, next time," was all Merissa said.

Samone's lips trembled. A hot tear splashed her cheek. But she lassoed the grief about to escape, her head high and determined.

Her words delivered were full of fevered promise.

"Absolutely, Merissa . . . absolutely."

And damned if she didn't mean that.

At 8:57 the next morning, Samone stopped by the receptionist's desk and retrieved her messages. The plain white envelope Darlene extended, eyes down, was not a surprise. Samone didn't have to open it to know what it was.

She checked her watch and said, "Thank you." She smiled an "It's okay" Darlene's way. Holding her head so high it hurt, Samone turned and walked away.

With great distress Darlene swiveled in her chair and looked at the office clock. Pulled out the clipboard with the time sheet attached. Wrote the date and, under it, the time: 8:57 A.M. Picked up the phone and called Harris.

"Harris."

"She's here," Darlene half whispered.

"Damn."

Darlene hung up the phone, fretful about this latest assignment. She had enough to do without having to clock Samone's coming and goings. Worse, Darlene didn't understand why Harris was out to get Samone.

She was the nicest personnel manager NBS had.

Samone always had a kind word or a smile for her. It was Samone who had taken her to lunch her first day. Samone never gave her last minute things to do and didn't get riled when she got a message wrong.

Samone gave her flowers on her birthday, always asked about how her son was doing in school, and complimented her when Darlene wore something nice to work.

Samone was the only one who treated Darlene as if she were somebody. She sure hoped Samone made it. Because Darlene liked her, a lot.

20

Samone was so grateful for the Christmas holiday, she didn't know what to do. For the last five weeks she had been busting her behind getting to work on time. Dragging, she got to Darlene's desk no later than 8:59 every morning. Nobody was going to force her out of a job. These days she liked what she did for a living, and not even Harris was going to take that from her. Samone was determined.

Now, with the air filled with the New Year's Eve spirit, Samone had other concerns as she squeezed Jon's hand in hers.

"Sure you can handle things?" she asked. The question was not a surprise; it had been in evidence since Jon picked her up. It had been asked without being asked in the uncertainty of her gaze, in the motion of her throat: her constant swallowing was a dead giveaway that she wrestled to keep something off her tongue.

It was New Year's Eve and they were on their way to Pat's house for a party.

"Why, 'cause I'll be the only white guy there?" They paused at the curb as the streetlight blinked *Don't walk.*

Samone looked around, cold, her breath frosty before her. "That and Max."

"Are you afraid of seeing him?" Jon asked, sensing the answer.

"A little."

The light changed and Samone stepped off the curb. Pat's brownstone half a block down never seemed so far away.

Ready or not, here we come. . . .

Pat stood back, one careful manicured hand on her hip. She gave them both a shrewd look before her lips moved to speak.

"Well, about time you got here. Hi, Jon."

Jon kissed her cheek with cold lips. "Thanks for the invite."

"No need to thank me. Sam is my best friend. She ain't supposed to be nowhere but at my party on New Year's Eve. Here, give me your coats. There's glasses of champagne on the kitchen table. It's like five minutes to midnight and I'm about ready to throw everybody out."

"I like that dress," Jon said, touching Pat's satin shoulder gingerly.

"Well, do you now," Pat replied, half-flattered.

"Yeah. Turn around. Let me see it from the back."

Pat laughed. Jon was such a flirt.

"Jon, you best behave yourself tonight. I mean it." Because when he got started, he wouldn't quit. Pat didn't know if he was half-serious or half-joking. Either way, she made it a rule with herself not to find out, no matter how cute he was.

"Samone, put a leash on that man and get your champagne. I'll catch you guys in a bit."

Samone took his hand. "Come on."

It was so crowded, people had to belly rub just to get from one place to the other. Dressing up seemed like a waste of time, because nobody could see anybody from the neck down.

Having made the kitchen stop, Samone and Jon squeezed their way into the smoky blue light living room. The music had been turned down to a soft garble, and everywhere people stood holding plastic glasses of cheap champagne, resisting the urge to sip.

In a corner, Samone waited, her eyes fast upon the TV screen and little else. She became aware of a different sort of energy buzzing toward her. And knew before she even looked that Max had found her.

She waved. Max waved back. With seconds to midnight, Samone took Jon's hand and started across the crowded living room.

"Hi, guys," she offered, this milestone now crossed.

"Hi," Carol-Anne piped up. "Happy New Year."

"Jon, this is Max and his friend Carol-Anne."

"Nice to finally meet you," Max stated truthfully.

Jon smiled, nodded, his mind racing as he took in the living legend. "Nice to meet you, too," Jon replied. "Feels like I've known you for years."

He was flexing muscle, and Samone knew it. She also knew that Max loved a challenge and would sooner take it up than let it slide.

"Be nice, guys," was all she said. But it was liberating to see the look in Max's eyes. Was worth all the sorrows he'd ever bestowed on her.

Samone smiled, self-conscious. "Well, if you will excuse us," she said, taking Jon's arm.

Just then someone turned the music down and the TV up, and the countdown was upon them. Ten . . . nine, eight, seven, six, five, four . . . three . . . two . . .

Even as Samone told herself it was wrong and dangerous, she could not stop looking at Max. Could not curtail the thoughts running through her now like wildfire.

In one second, the past will be gone. And it'll take you with it. I found somebody who needs me more than you ever will, the way it should be. So why am I scared, Max? Why am I afraid that the next second will take you away from me forever? Because I still love you. And I love Jon. God help me, but I love you both. . . .

"One . . . *Happy New Year!*"

Samone found herself kissing Jon, the touch of his tongue electric. Kissing Jon in Max's presence. She wondered about Max's thoughts as she did. Wondered if he understood, really understood, how it had all come to be.

Jon released her. Samone wiped lipstick off his lips, her eyes shiny, joyful. Her eyes danced toward Max, but Carol-Anne had his attention. Samone looked away.

Later, half in fun and half in tribute to a time gone, they started a *Soul Train* line. Pat was the first to go down, followed by Ray. After some coaxing, Jon made the journey.

The crowd, joyous and good-natured toward the only white guy in the place, cheered him on.

The first daybreak of the new year arrived in upper Manhattan without ceremony. No trumpets sounded, no bells rang. The only tangible proof that a new year had begun was the date on the newspaper and the new calendars on people's wall.

Physically it was just the day after yesterday and the one before tomorrow. It was just today doing time for the future, beyond a past already gone.

Over and done, Samone thought as she climbed out of bed, leaving Jon sleeping. Her mind was set on broiling bacon and whipping up pancakes. On which glasses she would use for orange juice and how much sugar Jon took in his coffee. Her mind was set on a shower and a clean nightshirt.

Set on last New Year's and the New Year's before that. Her mind was set on another part of town.

The call came around eleven that morning. Jon had

just gotten off the phone with his brother when it rang loud and unexpected.

Samone picked up. "Hello?"

"Samone, it's Mommy. Oh, baby, Uncle Chicken is dead—"

Samone frowned, her head shaking gently.

Uncle Chicken, born Oliver Lewis and only brother to Samone's father, was her favorite uncle. Uncle Chicken and his wife, Aunti, couldn't have any children, so Samone had become their "baby."

Uncle Chicken took Samone everywhere when she was coming up, Samone riding fast and free in the front seat of Uncle Chicken's Cadillac convertible. The wind whipping her fast asleep on the long rides home from Coney Island and Jones Beach. Her playmates envious, watching as Samone climbed into the big car with the let-down top, off to some fun place, like the 1964 World's Fair in Flushing Meadows Park or the Christmas show at Radio City. Most people got one daddy if they were lucky. Samone had two.

Uncle Chicken, dead? He can't be. He never said nothing about no dying. Nobody said nothing to me about Uncle Chicken gonna be dead come New Year's Day. He just can't be. Not my uncle. He would have told me. Come to me in a dream or appeared in the hall, just to say good-bye. He wouldn't leave me like this, all sudden and unannounced. He wouldn't . . .

"No, Mom . . . no."

"Yeah, baby, Aunti went to wake him this morning. Wouldn't move. Wouldn't wake up. Me and

Daddy are heading over there now. Aunti's waiting for the wagon. Uncle Chicken is still there.''

"No, Mommy, nooo.''

"I'm sorry. You all right?''

Her mother was, so she'd have to be. "Yeah. Jon's here.''

"You going over there? I called some other family, but right now I think it's just her and the police.''

"Yeah. I'll meet you.''

Samone hung up, stood perfectly still as her eyes grew wide with disbelief. Then she started shaking and couldn't stop. Didn't know how. All she knew at that moment was Uncle Chicken was cold, not breathing, and dead in his bed.

"What's wrong, Samone?''

She looked at Jon, her shaking more prominent. She tried to speak, but her tongue was locked.

Jon took her by the shoulder. "What is it?''

Samone blinked, the first time in many seconds. A tear trickled down her cheek. It was enough to loosen her tongue.

"Uncle Chicken's dead.''

She looked at him, expecting the horror to take him as it had taken her. Expecting him to moan against the injustice. But Jon only looked back in puzzlement.

"Who's Uncle Chicken?''

Samone blinked, the words out of his mouth confusing her. *What is he talking about? Uncle Chicken is my uncle. Why, he's the Cadillac Man. The magic carpet driver of my childhood. Why is he asking me this? Don't he know who Uncle Chicken is?*

And then the news arrived, abrupt and sobering. *No, he doesn't, Samone. He doesn't know Uncle Chicken at all. He has no idea.*

She pulled out of Jon's grasp, her movements jerky and without restraint, as though she were being pulled in too many directions at once. All Samone knew at that moment was she had to seek out people who could understand, people who knew who Uncle Chicken was. People who would know her loss the way she was feeling it.

"I gotta make some calls."

She left him and went to her bedroom. Closed the door. Didn't know why, only that she had to.

Jon followed, had just made it to the hall when the bedroom door closed shut. He blinked twice, startled.

He wanted to open the door, tell her that no matter who had died, he still loved her, because she needed to hear that now. But the closed door wasn't for the hallway or the tiled floor; it was for him alone.

Jon knocked, and when she didn't answer, he opened the door. He reached for her, but Samone moved out of his embrace. She was seething. She had to make some *calls,* and could she *please be alone?*

Everything inside of him wanted to tell her no. That she was acting irrationally, and if there was anybody she should be talking to, it was him. He studied the phone in her hand, waiting for her to put down the receiver.

"Samone."

"No, Jon. No." She turned her back, bent on privacy.

Jon granted her wish and left.

As Samone sat on her side of the unmade bed, her mind tried to decipher whom she had to call. *That's why I'm in here in the first place, right?* She had to call people, people who knew about her father's only brother. *Gotta call people . . . gotta call Pat and Ray . . . Max.*

Samone didn't stop to ask herself would it matter to him that Uncle Chicken was gone. Because somewhere deep inside, she knew it would.

She had not been wrong.

Must be bad news, Carol-Anne decided as she watched Max drop down onto the sofa. The phone was cradled tight against his ear. The collar of his leather bomber touching his chin, the keys to the rental car lying on the carpet where they had fallen from his fingers.

They had been on their way to pick up Carol-Anne's daughter from her mother's when the phone rang.

"No, Samone. No . . . when? . . . Where are you? . . . He is? . . . Okay . . . yeah . . . Don't cry, babe, please don't cry. . . . I have to see. . . . Yeah, later. . . . All right."

Max hung up and brought both palms to his eyes. Rubbed them for a long time before he looked up and saw Carol-Anne leaning anxiously against the wall. Max's eyes pulled away from her slowly, Samone's pain still with him.

"Samone's uncle just died," was all Max offered,

taking a few more seconds to regroup, to press back the need to mourn. He stood, sensing Carol-Anne's questions. Later, when he had time to really think, he'd tell her.

"Come on. Let's go get Nadia. Then I'll drop you. I have to go crosstown."

Carol-Anne, into day one of their new year, knew she had been pushed aside in the wake of this news. Beyond being Samone's uncle, he must have been a friend to Max as well, was what she kept on telling herself.

But then she kept on hearing her man on the phone with his ex-lover. Kept on hearing him call her "babe," like he called Carol-Anne only sometimes. It had sounded so natural and second nature, you'd have thought it really was Samone's name.

Carol-Anne's life with Max would always be filled with such moments, she decided, a new hurt moving through her eyes.

"He was a good friend?" Her voice had not been expected. Neither was her question. Max had not expected her to ask now.

"Let's go down, I'll tell you on the way."

"No, Max. No. Here and now. Let's talk now. This instant." She paused, took a breath. "You didn't hear yourself on the phone. Do you have any idea how I'm feeling? Listening to you talk to her like that?"

"Carol-Anne, don't do this. Not now. I got to get going."

"Get to where, Max? To pick up Nadia? That can wait."

"I have to get to Uncle Chicken's."

"Why? To do what?"

Max moved to answer, but he realized he didn't know. To do what? Console Aunti? No, Samone.

"They're like family to me. Can you understand that? Uncle Chicken was like my uncle. It's like my uncle died."

Carol-Anne's hand waved in front of her. "That's all you had to say, Max. Not just spew out directions like I know where you're going and why. A little consideration, that's all I'm asking. Don't assume I know your life like you know it. . . . I'm ready. You can drop me at my mother's. Me and Nadia will take the train home."

Her stinging words brought everything to a screaming halt. Made him stop. And think. Max slipped his keys into his jacket pocket. Extended his arms and gave Carol-Anne a humbled look.

Said, "I'm sorry."

But it wasn't enough for her.

Max continued, "You were right, again. There's no need for me to rush over there. What can I do there, anyway? There'll probably be enough people there already. I won't be missed."

She gave him an intimidating look. "Thought you said he was like an uncle to you. Like it was your uncle who died."

"He was, in a lot of ways, but that was all tied up in me and Samone being together."

"Well, at least you admitted it." She took a cleansing breath. "Samone calls, and your immediate instinct is to go running? You have to get past that, Max. You're my man now, not hers.''

She brushed by him, his arms, still extended, were pushed aside in her wake.

21

With Uncle Chicken dead, Aunti, two years retired, decided that 145th Street had seen enough of her life. She would go home, back to Georgia.

With Max making the funeral but not coming back to the house to eat and pay his respects to the living, Samone realized that his life was entirely without her now.

Max had not come to sit around and talk up old tales that had been buried right alongside of her uncle. He had not come to eat cousin Martha's potato salad or get a few slices of her mother's baked ham.

Max had lined up with the rest of the congregation and waited his turn to take one last look at Uncle Chicken. He had stopped at the first pew to pay his respects to Aunti, Samone's mother and father, some uncles, and then finally her.

He had given the men firm handshakes and the women cool, dry kisses on the cheek. Told Samone he would call her later and then left the church.

With Jon standing by her side the whole time, relatives looking on and commenting about the white man on her arm, Samone realized that her love life was now public knowledge.

Jon looked tired. There was a hollowness to his cheeks, and the sparkle was gone from his eyes. He looked like *his* uncle had died.

"You okay?" Samone asked from across the restaurant table.

"Nothing. Just tired."

But that wasn't it at all.

Like a thorn permanently in her side, that incident when she'd pushed Jon away pierced her every time she looked at him. For over a week Samone's apology got forced back in the wake of funeral arrangements and her own grief. Now, as they sat in the restaurant, she knew it was time.

"I'm sorry," she whispered, eyes full of pain.

" 'Bout what?" Jon asked punitively.

Samone's eyes glistened as she danced around the truth. "These last few days . . . been just crazy with grief. Haven't been too kind"—her eyes searched his—"and I just want to say I'm sorry."

Samone waited for forgiveness, for Jon's understanding. She felt on the verge of meltdown in her waiting. But Jon changed the conversation, and absolution was put aside.

"Taking a break."

"From?"

"New York . . . going home for a few days."

"California?" Just saying it hurt.

Jon nodded.

"When?"

"In a few days."

"Why?"

He looked at her. "Need some time away."

"From me?"

"Yeah . . . see my family. Feel the sun again."

Samone had needs, too. She needed Jon to take her hand, caress her cheek, something that would get her beyond the moment. She needed him to say he forgave her, that he was coming back.

"Just want a few days," Jon decided.

Samone needed to take back New Year's Day, her own insolence, her selfishness. She needed Jon to ask her along. To say he still loved her. She needed the love fire missing from his eyes for over a week.

"Okay?" he asked, taking up her hands.

Samone nodded, tears falling from her face like rain.

Samone lay in bed the morning of Jon's flight, staring at the ceiling. For the first time in over a week, the space beside her was empty, and Samone realized winter was no place to be alone.

She got out of bed and looked out of her window. The day was cloudy and the temperature below freezing. With her baseboard heaters struggling hard against the winter chill easing through her window frames, Samone wanted a shower, but just the thought of taking off her pajamas and being naked made her shiver.

So she brushed her teeth and made herself some coffee. Eyed the clock with anxiety.

Jon was halfway to California.

She didn't mind that he had gone and understood his need to get away. What she minded was Jon never accepting her apology. It tugged at her heart like a boulder.

Then there was that other bad-tasting thought that had gotten stuck in her mouth the moment he had told her he was going. The thought that had no intention of going away. The thought that only taking a flight to California and following him could dismiss.

That he was really going to see Yvonne.

And the more she considered this idea, the more she felt the need to hop a plane. The more she thought it, the less she could shake it from her head.

Jon had said he would call her when he got in, so Samone did what she thought she'd never have to do with Jon: she waited.

It was a four-and-a-half-hour flight. Give or take half an hour to get into the terminal, retrieve his luggage, and wait for his ride to show. Add another half an hour for the ride to his brother's house. She figured another twenty minutes for chitchat and unpacking. Roughly six hours.

His flight had left at 9:07. It was a little after 11:00 now. Idle hands were the devil's playground.

Samone cleaned house.

And when she was done, she braved the bad weather and went to spend some time with Pat.

The simplest of things could be missed, Jon realized as he maneuvered the Jeep Wrangler along the California coastal highway. The view was breathtaking. The coastline hugged the shore in rugged monolithic sheaths. The deep blue Pacific Ocean was a nonending jewel beneath the sun. The spray hitting the shore danced in a soft mist of luminous white.

Jon had started the excursion with no destination in mind, but as he rounded a sharp curve, he knew where his journey would end. He knew the house stood downshore. That it would look just as he remembered. Its beauty would still be specific, its appeal still alluring.

Without ceremony, Jon turned on his signal and pulled the Jeep into the driveway of his old Malibu home.

"Get over it," Pat was saying. Her hands moved quickly on Shamika's head; this last braid, nearly plaited, was taut beneath her fingers.

"Easy for you to say, Pat. Your man ain't three thousand miles away."

Finished, Pat tapped Shamika's crown, helped her up, and handed her the box of candy-colored barrettes. "Here, put these away. And then you can go play." Shamika had heard enough grown-up conversation for one day.

Shamika paused, searching her auntie's face. Knew any second her mother was going to send her scampering.

"You look beautiful, baby." Samone knew this wasn't what Shamika wanted to hear. Shamika wanted to hear that her auntie was okay, despite the anxious words that had rambled out of her mouth.

"Thank you."

Samone smiled pleasantly. "You're welcome. Now go on."

"If you ask me, you're just looking for trouble," Pat said, standing to gather the jar of blue pomade, the clump of loose hair, and the wide-toothed comb.

"Then why didn't he ask me to go?"

"Samone, last time I saw Jon, he was loving the hell out of you. Now I could be mistaken, but I don't think things change that much in a week's time."

"Yeah, you don't know Jon."

"You trust him?" Pat asked, the hair supplies bulky in her grasp.

"I don't know."

"Well, that's something different. Let me put these away. Be right back. . . .

"Now, talk to me," Pat said, settling on the couch. The chores of the day were finished, this time of rest and relaxation long overdue.

"It all started with Daryn."

"Who?"

"This blond chick. Me and Jon were sort of dating, nothing serious. Dinner. A movie here or there. Lunch, that sort of thing. Then one night we go to a

movie and afterward he wanted to go to this bar.
Some flaky joint where nothing but white folks hang
out. I didn't want to go. So I 'declined' the invite.
Well, he cops an attitude and puts me in a cab. He
meets Daryn the same night.''

''Yeah? So?''

''It took him like a whole month to tell me about
her.''

''Were you sleeping with him?''

''No.''

''He promise you anything?''

''No, but that's not the point, Pat.''

''Well, what is?''

''It's about trust. I mean, he was sneaking around
with her. We weren't sleeping together, so why the
big cover-up?''

''Maybe because he knew you'd be hurt.''

''I was not hurt.''

''Samone? Look me in my face and tell me you
weren't hurt when he told you.''

Samone took up the dare, but at the last minute her
eyes moved away. ''I wasn't hurt because he was
seeing her. I was hurt because he kept it from me.''

''Well, whatever the reason, you were still hurt. He
was probably just trying to protect your feelings.''

''Oh, yeah, right.''

''Look, Samone. You drove both me and you batty
with Max. I ain't going for no second ride.''

''Maybe you're right, Pat. I mean, he went through
a lot to get me. Hell, if he's up to something, there's
not much I can do about it.'' Life didn't come with

guarantees. Only thing she knew for sure was she would stay black and die. Anything else was a spin of the wheel. *And where I'll stop, nobody knows. . . .*

Samone stretched her spine, tension flowing away in the motion. She looked at her empty glass, suddenly thirsty.

"You got any more Cherry Coke?"

"A whole great big bottle in the fridge. Help yourself."

Samone made her way to the kitchen. Pat sat back and closed her eyes. Saturday night was one hour away. Next day was Sunday. Then it would be Monday again.

Time wasn't worth a nickel these days.

In half an hour she'd have to get up off her butt and go make dinner. Ray would be getting in from work soon.

"You and Ray and that nasty Cherry Coke."

Samone sat on the floor, the Persian rug inviting.

"This stuff is the joint. You just don't know."

"Tastes like cough syrup to me. But heaven help us if we run out. You'd think it was cocaine or something, the way Ray drinks it."

"I used to drink Coke Classic. Was all I'd drink. And then one day I was having a serious Coke fix and the store was out of the Classic, so I tried this. I ain't been back since."

"Nothing stays the same forever," Pat reminded her, reaching over to borrow a cigarette from Samone's pack.

"You right about that, Pat." Samone took one, too.

The house was silent save for the sound of steam moving through the radiators and the flaring of the flame as they shared a match.

"We really got to give this shit up," Pat said, looking down at the cigarette between her fingers.

"Yeah, we really do."

Pat took a drag. "We've been doing this shit too long."

"You right about that."

"Let's set a date," Pat decided, smoke moving hazily about them.

"Like for when?"

"Like for the first day of summer or something."

"Summer? No, not summer. How about fall?"

"Yeah, fall sounds good. . . . So we going to do this?"

"Sure. I'll mark my calendar."

Pat looked at Samone, and Samone looked at Pat.

"We some lying asses."

Samone laughed out loud.

Jon put on the emergency brakes, hopped out the side of the Jeep, and rounded the drive. A woman was on the deck, and Jon's heart thumped hard. He watched as she pulled a deck chair from the corner and positioned it so that the sun would be on her face.

For a moment he was unable to move. But he had come this far, so there was no sense in not going all the way. He began walking toward the deck.

The woman did not know him but didn't seem to mind his approach.

"Can I help you?" The book, ready in her long slim dark hands, was laid to rest.

"Oh. I'm sorry. I was looking for somebody else."

"Who?"

"Yvonne."

"Yvonne? Oh, she's not here."

"Is she coming back soon?"

"Week after next. She's on a buying trip. Is there something I can help you with?"

"You are . . . ?" Jon asked, incredulous that a stranger was sitting in chairs he had personally hauled home from Pier 1 Imports.

"Kiki," she offered, a bemused smile finding itself on her face. "Jon, right? I've seen pictures of you."

"Well, I haven't had the same pleasure."

"I'm Yvonne's cousin. House-sitting till she gets back."

"Nice to meet you," Jon said, wearied.

Suddenly the day grew too long. Jon found himself confused about why he was even there. Maybe he'd come to dwell in a love that was unselfish; to seek old comfort in the midst of troubled times. He didn't know what would have happened if Yvonne had been there, but his heart ached a little at the realization she wasn't.

"Are you thirsty? You look like you had a long drive," Kiki was saying, standing and putting aside her paperback. Ready to play hostess at the drop of a hat.

Apples didn't fall far from the tree. Kiki moved with the same ease and grace that Yvonne did. Even the way she pronounced her "r," carrying the hint of southern gentility just before the sound was finished.

A part of him did not wish to enter the house, the idea painful and full of emotional pitfalls. But he was thirsty, and something cold for the hike back was enough to tempt him through the patio doors.

The changes were subtle, but with his trained eye, Jon could see that Yvonne had taken away and added things to the kitchen that erased his presence and re-affirmed her own.

Even his coffee cup that used to hang under the counter was replaced with one Jon had never seen before. He wondered who it belonged to.

"Water? Orange juice? Ice tea?" Kiki was saying, her butt and not much else sticking out from behind the refrigerator door. Jon found himself watching it wiggle.

It could have been Yvonne.

"Heineken? Ginger beer? Milk?" Kiki went on, her hands busy moving glass bottles and waxed cartons, making sure that every choice was accounted for.

"Water would be fine," Jon decided. Anything else would cater to the need to sit and talk and ask questions.

So he stood by the counter and drank the water. Afterward and without thought, he walked over to the sink and rinsed the glass before setting it on the counter. Yvonne always insisted that was how glasses got broken, by putting them in the sink.

Rinse them and put them on the sideboard, she used

to tell him, in the same tone she used to ask that the toilet seat be put down and the garbage be emptied. There was a lot of Jon's life in the house, too much to count and remember. It was time to go.

"Thank you very much, Kiki."

"Don't be silly. This used to be your house, too."

He wanted to tell her that he wasn't just talking about the water, but he had already overstayed.

Kiki stood on the deck, watching, as he walked away. Her gaze was so intent, Jon could feel it.

Her voice rode the wind. "Any message for Yvonne?"

He was twenty yards away when she asked, as if she knew he wanted to leave a message but hadn't the courage. He pushed, looked off into the blue sky, and listened to the rustle at the shore. Lifted his head, smelled the brine in the air and the bright sun on his face.

Jon considered the isle of Manhattan and what it had cost him.

Any message for Yvonne? . . .

That's why he had come, wasn't it, to leave a message? No, Jon realized. He had come to feel the sun and taste the breeze. To stroll the beach and hear the seagulls keen.

Mostly he had come to leave his footprints in the sand, to reaffirm that once, this had been his life.

So Jon spoke, saying all that he could ever say.

"Yeah, tell her I said hi," and walked away.

*   *   *

Winter is no place to leave somebody.

It started snowing Saturday night. Helpless, people watched weather's brief move across the bottom of their television screens, waited for the full weather report on the evening news.

Sanitation trucks roared up and down the main streets most of the night, pushing away snow and spreading salt; but still the streets looked barely touched.

New York was having a snowstorm.

By Sunday, when Jon's plane was due to hit the tarmac at La Guardia Airport, incoming were being rerouted to Boston.

Jon had two choices as he got off the plane at Logan: sleep in the airport terminal, clutching his overnight bag as a pillow and his coat as a blanket, or taking Amtrak to New York.

Jon took the Amtrak. His train pulled in at 11:57 P.M., and he didn't even think about going above ground when he reached Penn Station. He took what he knew was still moving in the aftermath of the storm.

The A train.

Samone had lain down but couldn't sleep. It was now a little after midnight, and she didn't know where Jon was.

He had called her to let her know he was detoured in Boston and that he would try to get a train to New York. That was the last she'd heard from him.

She had watched the news till eleven-thirty and then switched on the Weather Channel, paying careful attention to the upper eastern region, where the storm was headed.

Tried to call Amtrak for verification, but the circuits were tied up. Samone rang his apartment, not really expecting an answer and getting none.

Just get back to New York, she thought, staring up at the gray night sky, her comforter about her tight.

A six-block walk. That's all. Six city blocks. Come on, Jon, you can do this.

The streets were so deserted, it felt like the end of the world. Traffic was nearly nonexistent.

Jon wished for a few things: a hat, some gloves. Even his rubber slip-ons would have been nice. He wished his overnighter had less packed away inside, and he wished where he was headed was closer.

By the time he reached the last block, his toes were numb beyond feeling and his ears felt boarderline frostbite. His leather shoes were so stiff with cold that they creaked. But he pushed on.

At the lobby, he looked up into the cold night sky, a little surprised that he'd made it. Then he opened the door and stepped inside. And the warmth rushed to greet him.

Samone came back with her comforter. She wanted him to get into bed, but Jon was afraid to lie down just yet.

"How are you feeling?" she asked, cautious and worried.

He smiled. "Cold."

"Oh, Jon. Why didn't you just stay in Boston till tomorrow?"

He tried to answer, but his teeth started chattering again.

"Never mind. You want something hot?"

He smiled again. "Yeah, you in a tight red dress."

"Stop joking, this ain't funny."

He nodded, agreeing. Stared at his feet and tried to wiggle his big toe. It would not move.

"No, I'm fine."

"You're not fine. Maybe I should call somebody?"

He waved her suggestion off.

"You sure?" Her eyes were drawn to his toes again.

He nodded yes, too weary to speak. Besides, he was getting drowsy. The warmth around him was acting like a tranquilizer.

"All right. I'm going to make you something hot." But as soon as she said it, and headed toward the kitchen, she remembered you weren't supposed to give something hot to a person who might have frostbite.

She'd make him some lukewarm milk with honey instead.

By the time Samone got back with the cup, he was dozing, his head falling upon his chest, his toes out before him. She went over and shook him.

"Jon? . . . Jon? Wake up. You can't go to sleep now."

He mumbled something as he tried to lift his head.

"No. Wake up. Come on."

She held his head with the free hand. Brought the lukewarm liquid to his lips. "Sip this. . . . Come on, Jon, sip."

He formed his lips over the edge but pulled back against the milky sweetness. It was enough to open his eyes.

"It's sweet."

"It's supposed to be. Now here. Hold the cup and take little sips." By the time the cup was half-empty, he was awake again.

Awake and looking at her. "Thanks."

"You're welcome. But don't you ever do nothing like this again? You hear me?"

"I wanted to see you."

"You could have seen me tomorrow."

"But I knew you were worried." He was looking at her, searching for her truth.

"Regardless," Samone said, taking her cup of tea and settling in the corner of the sofa.

"You were. I know you were." Those cat eyes were wide awake and upon her, forcing words from her heart.

"Well, maybe I was."

He nodded and closed his eyes for a moment, but only to gather his thoughts. Opened them and looked at her.

"I went to see Yvonne."

Samone's heart thumped so hard, she thought she heard it. Wondered if he had.

"Did you?"

"Yeah, I did. She wasn't there, though."

"Oh?"

"She was away on a business trip."

Samone brought the tea to her lips again and took a careful sip. "And if she'd been there? . . ."

Jon shrugged. "Who knows? Doesn't matter now. It was just a ghost I had to lay to rest."

"Was it?"

"What?"

"Laid to rest?"

"As much as Max is with you."

Samone nodded. "I've realized people don't stop being in your life when they're no longer there . . . like my uncle. That's what memory's really about, isn't it? To keep the dead things alive."

"As long as you remember they're gone. When you forget, that's where you run into problems. . . . Go look in the top of my bag. Brought you something back."

"What is it?"

"A typical white boy from L.A. gift, what else?"

"What? A Mazerati? A Diet Coke?"

"Just go look."

It was a big yellow one hundred percent cotton oversize T-shirt. The inscription read "My lover went to California and all I got was this lousy T-shirt."

"Did you buy this before or after you tried to find Yvonne?" Samone was asking, holding the shirt up to her shoulders, flaring out a leg to check its length.

"I bought it for you, that's all that matters."

Samone gave it a long thought. So long that the silence was complete. She nodded, in full agreement. Because, for here and now, it was all that mattered. Love *is*, when it is. . . .